SHARK'S HUNT

Shark Santoyo Crime Series #3

BY

BETHANY MAINES

Blue Zephyr Press
2661 N. Pearl, #360
Tacoma WA 98407

Cover art by **LILTdesign.com**.

ISBN-10: 1-7320863-6-2
ISBN-13: 978-1-7320863-6-4

TABLE OF CONTENTS

CONTENTS

SHARK'S HUNT

PROLOGUE

One Week Ago

Peregrine: The Ditch

"You sure about this, Peri?" asked Otto, looking around at the trees.

Seventeen-year-old Peregrine Hays checked her phone again. Outside the car, rain slapped at the windshield, battling the wipers and obscuring the line of trees along the road. She knew that Otto, her Ukrainian immigrant Lyft driver and occasional chauffeur, disliked trees and wildlife—he was always happier closer to concrete—but she couldn't quell her own nerves until she saw Lara. The app she'd put on the other girl's phone pinged Lara's location as only a little distance away. She just needed Otto to hang in a little further.

"Slow down. She should be just up ahead. It doesn't look like she's moving," said Peri.

Otto did as he was told.

"There," he said, pointing through the windshield wipers as they squeaked across the glass. Lara's car was parked on the side of the road, tail lights glimmering red in the early dusk.

"Pull up behind her," said Peri, pulling on the super-tight, trendy leather-look gloves she'd picked up recently. There were more holes to the gloves than glove, but warmth wasn't really the point. Not leaving fingerprints was the point. "Keep the engine running." She unclicked her seat belt and reached under her shirt. Pulling out one of her knives from the concealed band around her waist, she flicked it open as she exited the car.

She stood for a moment, watching the car for movement and telling herself that everything would be fine. Peri wasn't thirteen anymore. Things were going to be different this time. Lara wasn't going to end up like Vicki.

Taking a deep breath, she approached the passenger side, peering through the windows, looking for Lara. The car wasn't running, and the lights were starting to dim. The battery was dying. The driver's door was open. Peri went around to the driver's side. There was blood on the seat and on the grass beside the car—it looked black in the white light of Otto's headlights. She followed the trail down into the ditch by the side of the road.

The ground at the bottom of the ditch was soaked with blood. Lara's eyes were wide-open and staring at the raindrops as they hit her. Her blonde hair was in limp clumps. The bullet hole in her stomach was a dark flower on her shirt.

Peri reached out to touch Lara, seeing the echo of her thirteen-year-old hand stretching out to touch the ragged hole in Vicki's chest. It had seemed then like the hole was larger than Vicki, but this damage to Lara's body was discreetly hidden by her clothing. They were different, but somehow still the same.

Just as when she had been thirteen, Peri knew she should feel more upset. At the time, she had assumed that whatever drug they had given her was blocking her emotions because instead of feeling sad or afraid, all she felt was a cold churning anger. As she touched Lara, Peri could almost hear the clank of the handcuff around her wrist and feel the sticky blood spatter on her arm.

Peri knew that Lara wasn't Vicki.

Vicki had been Peri's best friend since they were five. Vicki had been the one who helped Peri limp home after the disastrous bike crash on Tillman's Hill. Vicki had been the one to help her work up the courage to give RJ a Valentine in fourth grade. Vicki was the first person she called to tell about anything. A hundred sleepless sleepover nights full of giggling. Endless summer afternoons in the backyard. Winter snow angels and throwing snowballs at boys, and then running.

Lara wasn't Vicki. But Lara had been someone's Vicki. Now someone had taken all of that away.

Just like someone had taken Vicki away.

"Vybliadok!" Otto was standing behind her with an umbrella and staring at what was left of Lara.

"Go back to the car, Otto," said Peri, standing up and putting her knife away. She'd tried it her uncle's way. She'd tried staying in the background—uninvolved and safe—and now Lara was dead.

Otto didn't move. Peri felt impatient at his paralysis. They didn't have time for the emotions that Lara deserved. She brushed past him and went back to Lara's car, and picked up the hot pink fur-covered phone in the cupholder. It had 911 already dialed, but the call had never been sent. She flipped through the apps and deleted the one that linked her phone to the dead girl's phone and dropped it back into place.

"Get back in the car, Otto," she said again.

"We shouldn't leave her here," argued Otto. "It's not right."

"No, it's not." Just like it hadn't been right to leave Vicki in that house.

"We should call the police. Someone should pay for this!"

"Someone will," said Peri.

"No," said Otto. "No, I'm not—" Peri turned around and looked at him. Otto backed up a step and shifted his grip on the umbrella nervously. He opened and shut his mouth twice, but nothing came out. "OK," he said, finally.

"Good. Now, get back in the car."

Someone was going to pay for this. Just like someone had paid for Vicki.

Tuesday ~ March 7

Shark: Rolling Thunder Lanes

"Look," said Marko, "I'm not worried about us. Profits are up, competition is down. Even the parole officers are happy because with the bowling alley running, everyone's got a job." They both looked up as the cold spring rain rattled against the windows with a sudden, fervent gust. "No, what I'm worried about is you spending more time in the city with no one to watch your back."

"I'm going to be fine," said Shark. They were sitting in a booth at the back of Rolling Thunder Lanes bowling alley, the headquarters of Shark's territory. At twenty-six, Shark was the youngest territory boss in The Organization. Shark suspected that this position was not a tribute to his ability to right the quickly sinking ship that had been the territory when he first arrived six months ago, but had much more to do with the fact that Geier, the leader of The Organization, knew that Shark didn't want it. Shark preferred his old, pre-prison position as an enforcer. But Geier preferred to make people unhappy, and it had amused him to make Shark tackle leading his most suburban criminal outpost. But now, finally, Geier was letting him come back in.

Which should at least get Shark's FBI handler off his back for a while.

"That place is a viper's nest," said Marko. "If you get whacked, what am I supposed to do? I can't go back there. I'm soft and lazy."

Shark laughed. He knew that Marko, with his classic Italian gangster look of slicked back hair, aquiline nose, barrel chest, and thick stomach, only appeared soft. He hid a bulletproof vest under loose shirts and a leg breaker's mentality under a genial facade. Shark also knew that Marko lifted weights every morning with the seriousness of a prison inmate.

"Thanks for your concern."

"Just think about taking Beef with you."

Shark had thought about it. He'd thought that Beef—the vegetarian, yoga pant-wearing, wise guy—would be an asset, even with the man bun. Unfortunately, Beef's presence would make meeting with the FBI more difficult. Maybe once he was settled?

"I'll think about it. Anything else?"

"Yeah, Domingo asked for five minutes of your time."

"If he needs more relationship advice, I think I may be all out."

"Did you see his junior prom picture? I think he may have surpassed us."

Shark chuckled as Marko waved Domingo over. The sixteen-year-old slid into the booth, looking nervous. He had recently cleaned up his hardcore gang look for a girl at school. Shark knew he was getting some crap for it from the guys, but it made him more useful to Shark and more likely to move up the food chain.

If either of them lived that long.

Considering that if Shark screwed up with either Geier or the FBI, his entire crew could be staring down a barrel or hard time, the idea of Domingo having prospects seemed a bit far-fetched. He wondered, more often than he cared to admit, if he shouldn't instead try to steer Domingo toward college and a job. Would he have listened when he was Domingo's age? Of course, when he was Domingo's age, he already had two bodies under his belt and his primary education had been the articles in Play-boy. At least Domingo was still in school, and would be as long as Shark could enforce it.

"What's up, D?" asked Shark.

"So I talked to Peri today, like usual."

Shark didn't react, even though the mention of her name made him want to flinch.

"Like usual?"

"Yeah, we have the same passing period. I go to math. She goes to English. She'll pass me a note from my girl and stuff."

"Domingo's girlfriend is not allowed to date, and her parents have spyware on her computer and phone," said Marko. "They are forced to write letters like Romeo and Juliet."

"More like low-tech email," said Domingo drily. "Anyway, usually Peri and I exchange notes and then we'll talk about school or whatever. But today..." He hesitated, clearly not comfortable. "She asked me to sell her five diamonds."

Shark frowned. He'd never known his girl to do drugs, let

alone buy them. Five baggies of coke could lead to serious time. "Doesn't she know that's felony weight?"

"That's what I said! I said that's intent to distribute if you get popped. And she said she knew. So then I was like, are you trying to get caught? And she said, yes. Only she had that smile. You know the one she gets when she's about to fuck someone up real bad?"

Both Marko and Shark nodded. They were familiar.

"What did you tell her?" asked Shark.

"I told her I didn't carry that on me and to hit me up after school tomorrow. I mean, I had it in my car, but I wanted to ask you. Because Peri usually has her shit wired, but she also usually doesn't mess with the substances."

Shark considered as Domingo verbally deliberated.

"So maybe I should do what she asked. But on the other hand, she is a friend and I don't want her to get jammed up." Domingo scrutinized Shark's face, looking for a clue.

Shark knew none of the gang could figure out why he and Peri weren't together. He hadn't made his visit from Peri's uncle public knowledge. But Al, the ex-special forces private investigator and grade-A asshole, had made his opposition to any relationship between Shark and his seventeen-year-old niece perfectly clear. Shark didn't scare easily, but Al had threatened to alert Shark's parole officer, Vivian Flood, to the relationship. Which would have been bad enough, except he was sleeping with Vivian, and she wasn't actually his parole officer. The tall, striking blonde was his FBI handler, and she had a mean streak a mile wide. If Vivian caught wind of Peri and her talents, he knew that she would go out of her way to stitch Peri up.

"I could just tell her I can't sell to her. But it's Peri. I'm pretty sure she can find an alternate source."

Shark couldn't fault Domingo's logic.

"Cut the weight," said Shark. "Cut it across all five bags, so they look and feel even, but make sure they're under the legal limit. No one ever weighs individual bags. That should get her what she needs, and if she gets jammed up with the cops, we can send in a lawyer."

Domingo looked relieved. "OK. Thanks!" He slid out of the booth with a smile.

"What do you suppose she's up to?" asked Marko after Domingo was gone.

Shark finished his Jack and Coke in one long swallow.

"God only knows," he said.

Shark: IHOP

Shark waited at the IHOP that was mid-way between the bowling alley and his new apartment in the city and tried not to touch anything. Fucking syrup residue was everywhere and the coffee tasted like it had been pressed through a gym sock. He was also annoyed by the sprinkling of shamrocks bouncing from the monthly special table topper. The calendar turned to March, and suddenly everyone was Irish.

Vivian Flood walked through the door wearing her standard look of contempt. Peri had once described her as the Valkyrie's naughty librarian, and the description was apt. Tall, stacked, and blonde with glasses and a button-down look, except for the stilettos she wore regularly, she looked like someone who enjoyed other people's pain. Shark knew from experience that this was true.

Today, she was accompanied by a man a little shorter than Shark with broad shoulders and a sour expression. Although, his expression might have been from having to spend time with Vivian. He looked about forty-five and was wearing jeans, a t-shirt, and a suit jacket. The jacket looked like a nod to someone's dress code. Vivian lowered herself into the booth, which was worth watching, and flagged down the waitress to order pancakes.

"You're not eating?" she asked.

"I don't eat this shit," he said.

"Not liking pancakes is un-American," she said.

"I like pancakes," said Shark. "I just don't like shit pancakes." Her companion cleared his throat, and she blinked, appearing to remember that he existed. "Ryan Holden, meet Shark. Shark, meet Ryan."

Shark stared. Ryan stared back.

"Ryan is working a tangential matter. He wants your input. I've told him that you won't have much to say on the subject, but he was insistent."

Shark's eyes flicked to Vivian. What the fuck was that supposed to mean?

"I want to ask about Fowler," said Ryan.

That's what it meant. How screwed were they?

"Vivian was there," said Shark. "I'm sure she can answer any questions you have."

ATF Agent Fowler had been stealing evidence—guns and drugs—out of a Federal evidence warehouse and selling them to the Scarecrow Jack mob, a rival to The Organization. He had also threatened to expose the fact that Shark had killed a few people while on the FBI's payroll. Vivian had not liked that. What Shark hadn't realized up until that day was that Vivian had a tendency to kill things she didn't like.

"Yeah, I'm not concerned about how things shook out. I'm looking into the Scarecrow Jack mob. I was hoping you'd have some additional information on Fowler's operation. Who his buyers were, that kind of thing."

Shark frowned. While he had dealt with Fowler, it had been

Marko who took care of the buyers. But Marko's investigation into the identity of the buyers hadn't gone further than the names on their driver's licenses. They might have gotten more if they hadn't had to dispose of the bodies so quickly, but the situation had not been conducive to investigation. "We didn't have any contact with them," lied Shark. He wasn't about to burn Marko over this shit. Particularly when Marko wouldn't have been involved if it hadn't been for Shark.

"Then how did you know that Fowler was dealing to the Scarecrows?" asked Vivian, looking amused. "Personally, I don't see a connection."

"The Scarecrows were dealing repackaged diamonds," said Shark. "All The Organization's stuff is stamped with red diamonds. The Scarecrows put a black heart over the top of it and resold them. Fowler was the only one who had access to a large quantity of Geier's product from a bust about nine months ago, and now that he's gone, the repackaged diamonds have dried up. It doesn't take much to connect the dots."

"Those are the dots I'm seeing," agreed Ryan. "But I need something more to move on. Clearly, Jack and Geier are rivals, and Geier has to be looking at how to stop the Scarecrows. I was hoping that as you proceed in Geier's organization, you might keep an ear out for anything that could help me."

"Back off, Holden," said Vivian. "I need him focused on Geier. He's my asset."

"I'm not trying to poach," said Ryan. "I'm just asking him to keep his eyes open." Shark watched with interest as they continued to argue.

Vivian was a decade or so younger, and although it seemed like they were doing the same job, Vivian was definitely acting like the boss. Meanwhile, Ryan was in the awkward position of needing a favor, but trying not to take her shit. He tried to assess how Ryan's presence might affect him. At the moment, not at all. On the other hand, it might be useful to have more than one FBI agent on speed dial. Vivian certainly wasn't doing him any favors.

"If I hear anything, I'll pass it on," said Shark, interrupting the flow. Vivian looked pissed. "Is there anything else? Because, seriously, I'm losing rep just sitting here."

"More information on Geier," said Vivian. "I keep saying it, and yet, it's like you're not hearing it."

"I hear it, but I can only do so much. I'll contact you when I have something."

"No, you'll make your assigned check-in, or I'm sending someone to arrest you in front of your friends. We'll see how your rep does then."

Shark took it with a smile. The screws always have to think they're winning.

"Yes, ma'am," he said, because he knew the *ma'am* would make her feel old. He got out of the booth and left before Vivian could figure out how to fuck him over some more.

Shark: The Apartment in the City

Shark's new apartment in the city was on the eighteenth floor in one of the high-rise buildings that Geier had an interest in. It was by far the best neighborhood that he'd ever lived in. It was so nice that the nearest pawnshop was over a mile away, and the rats knew to enter around back. Shark's handling of the Fowler incident had earned him the apartment and first choice of the furniture from the high-end furniture rental business that Geier owned. The stager, Jill Shapiro, was arranging his new belongings when he walked in.

Jill was a small, harried woman who appeared to be constantly sleep-deprived. He'd seen her a few times, but they hadn't spoken. His tour through the warehouse to pick out furniture had been with an assistant.

"You're Shark?" she asked as he walked in. He nodded. She looked him up and down. "You're younger than I expected."

"Based on what?" he asked.

"Based on your furniture."

"You don't approve of my choices?"

She laughed in a short bark. "As a designer? Certainly. As someone who is responsible for staging multiple locations, I'm annoyed. You're taking my best pieces."

"Sorry," he said, smiling.

"Why? You're going to have the best-looking apartment in this building. I wouldn't be sorry at all. What do you think of my placement of the dining table? I don't know where you found that, by the way. I'd forgotten we had it."

"You had it on display at the warehouse about five years ago," said Shark, eyeing the vintage Rohm and Haas, clear Lucite dining table. "I figured I'd want something that didn't block the view, so I got them to take it out of storage."

"Why didn't you try and get it back then?" Jill asked.

"They don't let you decorate in prison," said Shark.

"You're my couch supplier, aren't you?"

"Excuse me?"

"About five or six years ago, Mr. Geier got a screaming deal on several Le Corbusier couches. I could have used about three more in brown, but I couldn't ever get any more."

"Sorry," said Shark again. "Prison."

"Unfortunate. Well, let me know if you can get more, because right now you've got the last one." She pointed to the living room where the black leather and steel-framed 1960s couch held pride of place in the living room.

"I'll keep you in mind," he said. "But it's not likely." He didn't bother to add that the couches had led him to Francesca de Corvo, and when Francesca's father had landed chest-first on a pointed bronze sculpture, Shark had landed in prison. Since Francesca was currently Mrs. Some Rich French Guy, he didn't think the situation was likely to come up again.

Jill shrugged and gestured as if to say fate was what it was. She toured him through the apartment, getting his approval on locations and talking about rugs. His expensive furniture fetish had, as yet, not extended to rugs, so he let her do what she wanted. When she and the furniture movers finally left, he sat down on the couch and looked out the floor-to-ceiling wall of glass at the setting sun. He wondered what it would be like to have this all really be his.

Before going to prison, he'd clawed his way up the food chain of The Organization, from bag boy to dealer to enforcer. It hadn't been easy, and he'd spent way too many nights sleeping in rat and cockroach-infested hellholes. And when he'd finally made it to enforcer, he'd put a considerable amount of time and money into his own apartment. In the end, it hadn't mattered. The police had confiscated and auctioned off all of his furniture. Even his clothes had disappeared. When he'd come out, all he had left was what he'd entered prison in.

It had been a painful lesson. He'd tried to accept that possessions were temporary and that he couldn't invest emotions in them. But it was a struggle. He had been tempted not to decorate at all and go back to living with a mattress, a kettle, and a French Press, but he thought it would make Geier suspicious.

So he'd splurged. He'd ordered every fucking thing on his wish list.

He knew that even if he lived through this and the FBI really did hold up their end of the bargain—something he was less and less convinced of the longer he knew Vivian—that he wasn't likely to end up with a job that would afford him a twenty-thousand-dollar table. Which is why he had an offshore bank account that the FBI knew nothing about. However, adding to it now that he was back in the city, where Vivian would be keeping closer tabs on him, was going to be difficult. He wondered how much cash he could get into a safe deposit box before Vivian or Geier noticed. It was too bad he couldn't fit a Le Corbusier couch and a Lucite table in a safe deposit box.

An image of Peri floated through his head, and he swatted it away in irritation. Peri wasn't, couldn't be, part of the equation. Unfortunately, Peri draped across his damn twenty-thousand-dollar dining table was the kind of fantasy that tended to stick around.

In exasperation, he finally got up and went to find Geier at his restaurant, Kos. Shark was supposed to be re-integrating himself into the fabric of the gang, so he might as well start now.

Parking was a bitch at night, and Shark wondered who he'd have to kill to get one of the reserved spots in the lot across the street from the restaurant. He exited the car into a spitting drizzle that immediately found a way under his coat collar. Walking briskly, he dodged a meandering herd of bachelorettes as they took their inflatable penis down the street to the bar that was pumping out a grating remix of disco hits, and then was almost immediately blocked by two tourists who were staring at the posted menu of a café. He watched a grandmother, and obvious city native, shake her umbrella over the tourists and tried not to laugh when she ordered them out of the way. He drafted in the grandmother's wake and ducked down the alley that would take him to the back door of Kos.

Kos, named for a Greek Island, served a blend of Mediterranean and American comfort foods and catered to people who remembered when that had been exotic. White linen service and a French maître d' sold the top dollar prices and the chef—a man that Shark knew for certain had received his culinary training in prison—justified them with perfect meals.

Once inside, Shark jogged up the back stairs to the second floor which was where Geier held court.

Crease, Pompo and Guetta were playing cards as Geier did paperwork.

Crease, a smart, lanky black guy with diamond earrings and a bullet scar on his temple from where a bullet had creased his skull, was Shark's chief rival, although they both pretended otherwise. He was a few years older than Shark and they'd been in the same Juvie facility a few times. Shark thought of their working relationship as wary.

Pompo was a genial half-Asian guy who, having attained a level of affluence, didn't care to advance. Older than Shark by ten or fifteen years, and heavier by at least 40 pounds, he'd joined The Organization a few years after Shark and could be relied on to be mostly honest—mainly because their ambitions didn't overlap. Generally, they got along. The balding, round-faced Pompo had never been antagonistic and had occasionally been an ally. Shark wouldn't have called him a friend, but he didn't call him an enemy either.

Guetta was a morose and silent individual with a pallid skin tone and a weasel-shaped head who rarely voiced opinions and only showed any animation or emotion when burning things. Or people, as the case may be. Guetta had no friends. The three of them were Geier's top enforcers. None of them had specific territories, unlike Shark, who still nominally held the title of his little suburban fiefdom. That put Shark with one foot in the land of territory bosses and one foot in with the enforcers. As usual, he was not one thing or another. At least he was used to it.

And they were used to him. It was a relief to realize that he'd finally reached a point in his career where he didn't have to fight every second of the day to convince them to take him seriously.

"Room for a fourth?" he asked, going to the table after collecting a drink. Guetta said nothing, but pointed to an empty chair.

"The game," said Pompo, "is five-card stud."

Shark nodded, pulled out his wallet to buy his chips, and sat down to play. He remembered then why prison hadn't really been that much of a hardship. The routine was the same. Chow. Entertainment. Wait to be ordered into action. Hope no one tried to shank you. Repeat. Being on the outside didn't have the confined, claustrophobic pressure of too many people in one space, but the tingling need to watch his back was still there.

"Well, Shark, how's it being out of prison?" asked Pompo, with an easy smile.

Shark looked up, surprised at Pompo's choice of topic. Pompo had the pink cheeks that revealed he'd been drinking, but Shark knew better than to think anything of it. Pompo called it the Asian Blush and bemoaned the fact that he flushed as soon as alcohol hit his system. Shark supposed he hadn't been in the city enough to do the catch-up on the news chit-chat with Pompo, but prison seemed like old news at this point.

"Better food," said Shark, deciding to simply respond to the question.

Pompo chuckled. "Now come on. The lights, the air, the free-range titties? You can't get that in prison. If you're not enjoying life on the outside, you're not trying hard enough."

"I don't know, there was a guy in the next block over that had pretty big titties. He never wore a bra," said Shark, which made Crease laugh.

Pompo tsked. "You're too young to go all sour like Guetta here. You should go out with some of my guys."

"Too young? How old do you think I am?" asked Shark. Apparently, during Shark's absence, Pompo had become an old man.

"Twenty something?" Pompo squinted. "Who can tell with you Sorta-ricans?"

"Yeah, I know what you mean. It's like Asians—are they forty or 110?"

Pompo heaved a chuckle, his belly bouncing. "My point is that while you're more than welcome at my strip club, I no longer participate in the active crap you people call dancing these days. You should go out with some of my crew. They can show you a good time. Devonte, Malone!" Pompo snapped his fingers at two younger guys who were slouching against a wall, ignoring each other for the entertainment of their phones. "You can take Shark out sometime this week, can't you? Poor guy is just out of prison and been spending all his time in the suburbs with soccer moms and shit. Needs to remember what a girl's ass looks like."

Malone blinked. "Yeah, sure, man."

Shark looked at Malone—he was wearing a filthy ball cap,

and his pants sagged to the point where Shark was willing to bet that he couldn't run. He looked like an idiot. Devonte was a multi-ethnic-looking kid who was too skinny, but had better-fitting pants than his friend, and was watching Shark with a wary expression that spoke well for his intelligence.

"Sure," lied Shark. Neither Devonte or Malone looked like they believed him, and that was just fine.

Geier hung up the phone and walked to the card table.

"Shark, what are you doing? If you start playing well with others, you'll lose your reputation."

"It's OK," said Shark. "I'm planning on taking all their money."

Geier laughed and then turned his attention to Pompo. "You're on with the Reyes Brothers on Thursday. Usual setup."

Pompo nodded.

"I won't be needing any of you for the rest of the evening," said Geier to the room. There was a general chorus of affirmatives and the start of a slow shuffle to the door.

"You're the Reyes liaison? How'd you manage that?"

"I'm good at taking drugs," said Pompo, cryptically.

The Reyes Brothers were South American suppliers and were notorious for only working with certain people. At the time Shark had gone to prison, Geier had still been handling the Reyes buys himself. The fact that he'd managed to shuffle the duty off to Pompo was a feather in Pompo's cap.

Shark nodded his kudos, and Pompo smiled. Shark began to wonder how he could take Pompo's job. He probably would need to be better friends with Pompo. That meant he really was going to have to go out with Malone and Devonte. He glanced over at the pair. Devonte had wandered off, but Malone was obviously playing Candy Crush. Life on the outside left a lot to be desired.

Wednesday ~ March 8

Peregrine: Wednesdays with Domingo

Peri closed her locker and waited for Domingo. He brushed off his friends and came up next to her.

"We're good to go," he said. "Meet me at my car after school."

"You mean, you talked to Shark and he said yes," said Peri. Domingo's face froze, clearly uncertain of what to do next.

"Yes," he said, whether from fear or surprise, she wasn't sure.

"Nice of him to give you permission to take my money," said Peri.

"Peri," protested Domingo, reaching out for her arm. "It ain't like that."

"Don't even start, Domingo," she hissed, staring at his hand. He withdrew it without making contact. He looked worried and she took a deep breath. "Yeah, your car," she said in a more normal tone. "After school. See you there." She added a smile to let him know everything was fine. He smiled back half-heartedly before turning to head for his math class. She continued on to English class and found Mrs. Edison watching her from the doorway. She gave the teacher a smile because that was what was expected, and besides, she genuinely liked Mrs. Edison.

The teacher nodded back with a measuring look. Class started and Peri realized that they were still droning on about poetry. Peri settled back in her chair and prepared to tune out. At the end of class Mrs. Edison returned the previous week's assignment—a poem about love—to the students.

Peri accepted the paper and then felt herself flush bright red. The paper was marked *D*. She had never in her life received a *D*. Under the large mark were the dreaded words: SEE ME AFTER CLASS.

Peri waited until the rest of the class shuffled out and then approached the desk.

Mrs. Edison wore her hair in natural curls and liked African print inspired scarves. Peri always appreciated her colorful look in contrast to the other teachers who seemed to be locked into blacks and grays. Today however she found herself hating the English teacher's orange and green scarf, and pretty much everything else about her.

Mrs. Edison looked up with a questioning look in her eyes. Peri held up the paper with the scarlet mark of shame.

"Ah," said Mrs. Edison. She got up from the desk and closed the door. "So," said sitting back down at the desk. "Love poetry. Clearly not your favorite assignment."

"Yeah, but a *D?* I followed the format."

"Oh, you followed it to a *T.* But to be perfectly honest, that was the worst poem of the entire group. And I'm including Julie Ciccarelli's poem *Love is Fun!*" Mrs. Edison hit Julie's Valley Girl inflection perfectly and Peri smothered a laugh. "Maybe you should have asked your friend Domingo for help."

"Excuse me?" Peri felt a chill of anger. Was Mrs. Edison threatening Domingo?

"You pass notes for Ashley and Domingo, don't you? You must have read some of his work."

"No!" Peri was horrified at the invasion of privacy.

"Oh, you should," said Mrs. Edison. "He's really very good. Occasionally filthy, but incredibly talented."

"And when have you read them?" demanded Peri.

"He composes on his phone and then copies them out in my class after he's done the reading. I sneak looks over his shoulder."

Peri didn't know what to say to that. "Shouldn't you be ratting them out?" she asked after a moment. "Or stopping him or something?"

"Not only has a student suddenly started doing the readings and homework assignments, he's also composing beautiful poetry. Why on earth would I want to discourage that?"

Peri shrugged. "OK, fair enough, but I'm still not asking him for help. It was just a stupid… assignment." Peri reigned in her urge to add *fucking* to the middle of the sentence. Mrs. Edison looked like she was well aware of which word had been omitted.

"Is this about that boy?"

"What boy?"

This was the longest conversation they'd had in four years of high school. She was surprised by the teacher's insight and annoyed that Mrs. Edison was capable of surprising her.

"The good-looking one with the car. I saw you talking to him, oh, I don't know, around Halloween?"

"What makes you think this is about him? Maybe I just don't like poetry."

Mrs. Edison gave her a get real look.

"Because he's the only boy I've seen you look at other than Trey. Not that the boys don't try, but you look right through them. Poetry only sucks this hard if you're mad at the topic."

"I'm not talking to you about this," said Peri, struggling to collect her bag.

"Are you talking to anyone about it?" asked Mrs. Edison. "Because I don't think you are, and I think you should."

Peri felt an unexpected prickle of tears behind her eyelids. Abruptly, she threw her bag down and flopped into the chair by the teacher's desk.

"He ghosted me, OK?"

"Oh, ugh." Mrs. Edison looked sympathetically horrified. "Did you sleep with him?"

"Mrs. Edison!"

"What? I'm just trying to assess where we are on the trauma scale."

"Well, we didn't. I was totally going to." She saw the teacher's next question forming. "And yes, I'm on birth control. Depo-shots. No fuss, no muss, no accidents, and no evidence. Anyway, we had a date and then he cancelled. And then he ghosted. No explanation. He was just gone."

"Did you try to talk to him in person?"

"I know when I'm being ditched. I'm not going to go make a scene. It's not like we had anything formal."

"I'm sorry, honey. That really sucks."

"That's it? That's all you've got?"

"What? I can't fix this. I'm an English teacher, not your fairy godmother. If you were over twenty-one I'd take you out for drinks and then we could go slash his tires."

"That's not a good idea," said Peri.

"I'm glad you think so," said Mrs. Edison. "Very mature of you."

Peri didn't bother to correct her. Not slashing Shark's tires was more a matter of not wanting to get shot than of any maturity on her part.

"I just wish I knew what I did wrong," said Peri.

"You didn't do anything wrong," said Mrs. Edison confidently.

"How do you know?" demanded Peri.

"Peri, if your behavior didn't change, then there was some other factor in his decision. Maybe he just had more time to consider whether or not sleeping with a seventeen-year-old was a good idea." Peri rolled her eyes. "Sorry, I'm trying to rein in my judgment, but it's hard. Anyway, my point is, it's not your fault he's a jerk."

"You know, what the worst part is? He's one of the few people I could ever just talk too. And I miss him. I'm fucking pissed as hell, but I still miss him and his stupid face."

"Yup," said Mrs. Edison, looking incredibly sympathetic. "Welcome to suck town."

"You're so not good at this," said Peri.

"Sorry," said Mrs. Edison. "But I can at least offer you the opportunity to re-do your poem and get a better grade."

"Mrs. Edison, I don't really think that's going to help. I don't have a love poem in me."

"Sure you do. It's called: *I Fucking Hate You, But I Still Miss Your Stupid Face.*" She pushed Peri's paper back across the desk. "Stick less to the format, stick more to emotional honesty. That's poetry."

Peri took the paper back with a sigh.

"And Peri, you do know that if you need help, you just have to ask, right?"

Peri laughed. She hadn't meant to. She could see that Mrs. Edison was serious. It wasn't Mrs. Edison's fault that she was utterly wrong. If she blanched at the idea of a seventeen-year-old having sex, she wasn't going to make it through the rest of the check-list of things Peri needed help with.

"Thanks Mrs. Edison. But I'm OK. Just in a funk."

After school, she dutifully walked across the parking lot to Domingo's car. Since Shark's takeover of Blue Street, Domingo always backed into the space that was closest to the exit. She suspected that Shark was responsible for the overall upgrade in strategy for the entire gang, but Domingo seemed to take his word as gospel. Peri figured that for his line of work, there were worse messiahs—Shark's shit was always wired.

Domingo was sitting on the trunk of his car, looking pleased with life. She scanned the parking lot—Ashley was waving from the back of Regan's beat up Corolla as it pulled away. There must have been making out.

Peri hopped up on the trunk beside Domingo and looked back at the school. The school had always struck Peri as the definition of bourgeois. It wasn't ever going to compete with the nearby private schools—the income base wouldn't support that—but caring teachers and an active booster club really tried. Striving was the word that came to mind when she looked at the collection of two story brick buildings that wanted to look like a better class of school but couldn't quite pull it off. Or maybe that was just how she felt about high school—always trying and never quite making it.

"You two are barf-tastic," she said, as the Corolla let out a loud squeak of its inadequate horn.

"Don't hate the playa," he said. "Hate the game."

"I will barf on you, playa," said Peri. "You got something for me?"

He slid a binder out of the stack of books next to him and passed it to her. She scooped the five bags out of the interior pocket and slid them into her pocket behind the cover of the binder, before handing it back with a wad of cash.

"Are you sure about this?" asked Domingo.

"Worried about me?" she asked, amused.

"I'm not the only one," he said.

She took a deep breath. Her anger at Shark, that had been within easy grasp for the last few months, seemed to have suddenly vanished. She didn't know what to do without it.

"Is he happy?" she asked.

"I wouldn't know," said Domingo. "You know him. When it comes to poker faces..."

"Yeah. Is he seeing anyone?"

"I heard a rumor he was boinking his PO."

Peri felt a searing stab of hatred for Vivian Flood, the tall, blonde, and gorgeous parole officer. How was she supposed to compete with that?

"But if he is," continued Domingo. "I don't think it's serious."

"Why not?"

"Can't be serious about someone you hate. He may have a poker face, but he's not trying very hard to hide that."

Peri nodded. "Thanks, Domingo," she said, sliding off the car. "And do me a favor, don't tell him I asked about him, OK?"

Domingo nodded. "Let me know if you need help with anything," he said.

She laughed. "You're the second person today that's made that offer. Have I got a damsel in a dress look going on, or what?"

"Nah," said Domingo, laughing. "It just occurred to me. I mean, I got a gang behind me. It must be hard being an independent."

"It's the way I like it," said Peri with a shrug. "Thanks for the offer, though."

Peregrine: The Thing about Tits

Peri was waiting at the bus stop when Trey called. She hated waiting for the bus. She spent most of her time getting from place to place as fast as possible. Riding the bus was like strapping the hare to the tortoise. She knew she could afford calling for a cab or a Lyft, but it would have been out of the norm for a high-schooler, so she forced herself to ride the bus. That was the discipline of staying beneath the radar. Not that she didn't routinely deface the shiny veneered smile of Preston Peccary, the realtor who had ads in every bus stop around town. She might have to ride the bus, but that didn't mean she had to like it.

"Hey Babe!" Trey exclaimed cheerfully when she picked up.

"Hey," said Peri, smiling. California agreed with her boyfriend. Or maybe it was the stable home life of his cousin's house. "Well, did you get it? Are you calling to brag?"

"No, not yet. Internet says the letters won't arrive until the end of the month. I'm so sweating. What if I don't get accepted?" Going to Stanford was Trey's dream. He had the grades, talent, and the sob story to be a shoe-in, but he was still sweating— which was so like him.

"Then you'll go to UCLA with the rest of the peons."

He laughed. "Hey, the reason I'm calling, though, is that I totally had a brain wave."

"Oh dear," said Peri.

"Hey, I have the best ideas."

"Mmm," said Peri, choosing not to commit to an actual response.

"You're never going to let me live down broccoli chocolate cake, are you?"

"No, I'm not."

"Anyway, so last month was my birthday,"

"I'm familiar with your birthday," said Peri. "I virtually attended your birthday party, remember?"

"Yes, but what if you really attended your *own* birthday party?"

"Come again?"

"OK, that didn't come out right. So I'm eighteen now. Which, before you say duh, I should point out that aside from the wonderful right to be drafted, also means that I get the insurance money from my uncle."

"Oh," said Peri. Trey's mother had taken out a million-dollar insurance policy on her brother and set Trey as the beneficiary, then she'd asked Peri to make sure it paid out. Peri, with Shark's help, had delivered, but the result had been that Trey had moved to California when his mother's death from cancer had left him orphaned.

"So I was thinking, that what about next month when it's your birthday, that I fly you out for the weekend? Isn't that the best idea?"

"Uh," said Peri. "Um, yes? I don't know. I'd have to check with my mom. I hadn't even thought about what I was going to do for my birthday."

"Well, start thinking about it! I've got the cash and I want to spend it on you!"

She felt her phone vibrate against her face. She pulled it away and saw that Emma had texted.

Got an errand from Javelina. Can you come with?

"Well, maybe you should save your cash for Stanford," said Peri practically.

"And maybe you should pack your swimsuit and get out here."

"I'll think about it. Hey, my friend Emma is texting, and I think I can get a ride with her. Can I call you back?"

"Sure! But seriously…"

"Yes, I hear you. I will seriously think about it," she lied, before hanging up and texting Emma back her reply and location.

She waited for Emma and skimmed through social media, trying to occupy her brain and not think about Trey, her birthday, or all the attendant emotions that went with them. She kept thinking that she'd find a quiet time to do the thinking that those subjects seemed to require, but as soon as she found a moment she immediately found a vastly more important chore to do. Thinking about Trey and graduation made her sweat. She'd rather face down another biker gang than have to make some sort of assessment of her relationship or figure out what she wanted to do about her birthday.

"Thanks for coming with me," said Emma, as Peri climbed into her 1990s BMW. Peri nodded. The petite Korean girl looked nervous. "I just really hate going alone. Usually they send Lara with me, but you know…"

Lara was dead.

The police were calling it a road rage incident. That was the only explanation anyone could come up with as to why a sixteen-year-old girl would be shot to death in a ditch on the side of the road.

They rode in silence. Finally, Peri decided that subtle wasn't going to work if there was no conversation to subtly work with.

"What do they have on you?" she asked.

"What? What do you mean?" Emma's brown eyes widened nervously.

"I was friends with Lara, too," said Peri. "They caught her using weed. She said that's how come she had to run their errands. What do they have on you?"

"Dexies," said Emma sadly. "They caught me with some red Dexies. Which, I know they're illegal, but it's so totally unfair. I have a problem. I should be able to take medication."

"Problem?"

"My ass? I'm not blind. You don't have to pretend. I know I'm fat."

"You're not fat and you do know that the red Dexies are just speed, right?"

"Whatever," said Emma.

Peri shrugged. Body dysmorphia was real.

Emma followed the directions to a house in a gated enclave. Following Ms. Javelina's directions, she punched in the code and soon they were pulling up at the most unkempt house in the neighborhood. The front yard was overgrown and the front door paint was peeling.

Peri put on her gloves and helped Emma take giant plastic bags out of the trunk. She took a quick peek at the contents— they were full of smaller baggies of dope, all marked with black hearts. No one answered their knock on the front door. After a moment, Peri opened the door and went inside.

Through the front hall was a sunken living room leading out onto a deck and pool. In the living room the remains of several weeks' worth of partying were scattered around, including three junkies laying on couches and watching an enormous high-def TV. Pot brownies with little sugar shamrocks on top had been placed on a tray on the coffee table. They actually might have looked tempting, but Peri heard a quiet rustle down the hall and thought she saw the flicker of a mouse tail. No food was safe food here. Out by the pool there were more people, laughing and sunning themselves in the weak March sunlight and forest of heat lamps.

"We're looking for Tommy," said Emma.

"Making a sandwich," said one of them without moving his head.

"Stay here," said Peri. "I'm going to go use the bathroom."

She went down the hall and began a quick inspection of the house. It was mostly empty of furniture. Someone had been selling pieces off she guessed. She found an office and inspected the stack of mail. It was mostly junk mail and to the resident of— more evidence that whoever the owner of the house was, they weren't living here. She checked the time. She had left Emma alone too long. She made her way back to the living room.

Emma was not in there. Peri scanned the room, feeling a

swell of panic, but finally spotted her out by the pool. Emma was sitting awkwardly half off a man's lap. He was blonde and attractive in a skinny, stringy-haired Kurt Cobain kind of way. He had an arm around Emma and was offering her a syringe. His burn set up was on a table in front of him. It looked like heroin.

"No, Tommy," Emma was saying. "I don't think…" But her half-hearted efforts to push Tommy away were not effective and the needle moved progressively closer to her arm.

"Hey!" said Peri. "It's a pool! I love pools!" She ripped off her t-shirt and, waving it over her head, grabbed Emma by the arm and threw her into the pool. Then she grabbed the next guy and tackled him into the pool. "Woohoo!" she yelled as they hit the water. There was a wave of laughter and a few more partiers followed suit.

Peri grabbed Emma, whose face was burning pink as she tried to cover her chest; it could be clearly seen through her wet t-shirt that she wasn't wearing a bra., Peri pulled Emma out of the pool and then through the house and back out to the car.

Peri pulled on her own wet t-shirt and got in the driver's seat. "Give me the keys," she said, snapping her fingers. Emma handed them over with a shaking hand.

"I can't believe you did that!" she gasped as Peri put the car in drive.

"Well, if you want to go back and take his shitty heroin, I'm sure we can do that."

"No!" Emma held one hand up to the heater while holding her other hand over her chest. There was silence in the car as Peri navigated her way back to the freeway.

"I can't believe everyone just saw my boobs," said Emma, huddling into a sopping ball in the corner of the passenger seat.

Peri shrugged. "They're tits. Everybody's got them."

Emma gaped at her, seemingly at a loss for words. "But these ones are mine!" she finally wailed.

"Well, if the choice is between having some junky inject you with heroin and flashing your tits, then the answer should always be tits. Don't you think?"

"I think there should have been a different way to handle it," said Emma, striving for dignified.

"Like you were handling it?" Emma sank further into herself.

"Tell your parents," Peri said, breaking the silence as they pulled up in front of her uncle's house.

"What?" Emma looked shocked.

"Tell your parents you've been over-doing it and you think you have a tiny problem. That you need to go do a little rehab. Probably outpatient."

"I can't do that," said Emma, trading places with Peri and moving into the driver's seat.

"If you tell your parents then Javelina hasn't got shit on you and you can stop doing this. Think about it."

Emma looked unconvinced. "I'll think about it," she said and slammed the door.

Peri looked after her. "No, you won't," she said, and then shivered in the March wind.

Peregrine: Al's Apartment

Once inside her uncle's apartment, Peri took a shower and then pulled on her drill team workout gear while her other clothes dried. She knew Al would have a little aneurism over the short shorts and tank top, but she still hadn't replaced her bag full of workout clothes that she usually kept in his front closet. Mostly because they had actually been jogging together, which was weird. It was fun having sober Uncle Al around. Weird. But fun.

She pulled a stick of gum out of Al's gum/condiment packet drawer and popped it in her mouth as she dumped out the contents of her backpack onto the kitchen table. She shoved the school books back in and then fished out the baggies she'd gotten from Domingo as well as her crumpled old make-up bag, which today was full of cash.

Then she went to the cupboards and found a glass and filled it from the faucet.

As usual when she was alone in Al's apartment, she checked the lone bottle of Elijah Craig bourbon in the cupboard. The dust ring was undisturbed. The secret mark on the bottom was still there. Either Al was better at hiding his drinking than she was at catching him, or he really was sober.

Peri was aware that had Al been sober when she started her after school activities he probably never would have given her any of the training she needed. And she could tell that the longer he was sober, the more he was uncomfortable with the shit she was up to. Which was unfortunate because it meant she had to be a lot more careful around him. She loved that he was actually present and healthy, but he was too damn smart when he wasn't drinking.

She cranked the crappy ancient radio on the kitchen counter, switched from Al's oldies station to Top Forty and sat down to count her cash. She'd grabbed all the petty cash in the first two stuffed animals on her shelf. She kept swearing she would organize her money, but considering that her retirement and college accounts had a different revenue source, she generally didn't bother to count her income until it began to annoyingly protrude from Winky Pegasus's butt.

She was halfway through counting and blowing an enormous bubble when Al walked in.

"What the fuck is this?" he demanded. She popped her bubble with a loud snap.

"Drugs," she said, pointing to the clear baggies, each with a single red diamond stamped on one side. "Cash," she said, pointing to piles of hundreds.

"You do this on purpose to fuck with me," said Al.

She grinned.

"Yeah, a little bit."

"Seriously, where did you get all this cash?"

"I don't work for free," said Peri with a shrug.

Al scanned the table. "That's at least five grand."

"I hope so," said Peri. "I need to buy a car. That's enough to buy a car, right?"

"You can't drive," he said.

"I can," she said. "I've been driving you around for years. I'm just not very good at it."

"I meant that you don't have a driver's license," said Al, refusing to engage on the fact that Peri had been pulling him out of dive bars for the last four years.

"I have, like, three," said Peri.

"You have three fake ID's?"

Peri stared at Al. She actually had five, but she thought he'd known about at least three. But he seemed surprised. Which meant that she'd just unnecessarily admitted to three.

"I don't know. Maybe it's just two. One of them was such a hack job I couldn't believe it worked on anyone. I might have tossed that one. Why are you surprised? Did you think I had fake ID's for my own entertainment?"

Al took a deep breath. "Peri, why are there drugs in my house and why do you need a car?"

"Because I can't get caught with drugs if I have no drugs. And I can't get blackmailed into doing mysterious errands all over town if I don't have a car."

"You want me to drink, don't you?" He dropped his coat over the back of a kitchen chair and took the pistol out of his shoulder holster, placing it, and the extra magazine, on the table. "OK, I'm going to go change and when I come back out you're going to tell me what the fuck is going on."

"Cool," said Peri blowing a bubble and going back to counting.

"And for God sakes, put some clothes on!" he barked over his shoulder on his way to the bedroom. "You look like a Vietnamese prostitute."

"Why do you know that?" she yelled after him. He was silent. "Seriously, it's either racist or proves you have some experience in that department. Which is it?"

"Fuck you!" he yelled back, which made her laugh.

Al came back out in his faded Marine Corps sweats. She made a mental note to get him a new set for his birthday. His were starting to get ratty.

"Did you eat?" he asked, tossing her an extra pair of sweats and going to the fridge.

"Nah, I have to go home in," she checked her phone, "about an hour. Mom will make dinner." She put the last hundred in a pile and pulled on the sweats Al had given her.

Al pulled out a take-out box and sniffed it before putting it in the microwave. "What was the total?"

"Four thousand, eight-hundred, and sixty bucks."

"How do you have five grand? I don't have five grand."

Peri gave him a stare of disbelief. Who was he kidding?

"You have fifteen grand under your bed in the gun safe."

"That's my bug-out cash. I don't have five grand to just go buy a car with. Also, stop searching my place. I thought you were helping people and stuff. I didn't think you were taking them to the cleaners."

Peri decided that she probably shouldn't tell him about the

other three stuffed animals. And the pot brownie in the *Hello Kitty* make-up bag probably should never, ever, be brought up under any circumstances.

"I don't search your place. You had me pull out a hundred bucks last month. And I don't charge everyone," said Peri. "Some kids really need help. Other kids are just fucking stupid, and there should be a price for stupidity. I never charge more than they can afford." She didn't mention the occasional non-high-school-related contracts she took on. They paid more, but he wouldn't approve of the increased risk.

"And what do you do if they don't pay up?"

"They always pay up," said Peri. "One way or another. Also, I always get the cash up front."

"OK, the scary implications of that statement aside, that's still a lot of cash and a lot of problems to solve."

"Why do you think I have no free time? But aside from that, I have no bills. It's not like I'm paying for rent or insurance or whatever you people do. Anyway, can you help me buy a car?"

"Why do you need a car? You haven't needed one before now."

"Happy Place," said Peri, as if that explained everything.

"We talked about this," said Al. "You've been all over the Happy Place Youth Center. We don't have anything to take to the cops."

"Well, aside from the creepy pervoid vibe—"

"That I can't take to the cops. I've got to have something tangible," Al reiterated, and Peri rolled her eyes. They'd already had this argument multiple times.

"They're blackmailing kids. I went with Emma today."

"Which one's Emma? Is she on the drill team?"

"No! We don't even go to school together. I met her at Happy Place." Peri decided not to mention Lara. She thought he wouldn't agree to the next part of the plan if he knew that the threat level was death. "They caught her with red Dexies and now she does errands for them."

"Errands?" he repeated, catching implied air quotes.

"She delivered about a kilo of coke to some heroin junkie up in Pomona Heights."

He rumbled something inarticulate in surprise. "OK, find a kid who'll testify, and we can take it to the cops."

"I'm not going to find anyone," said Peri. "I can't even get Emma to tell her parents that she needs help."

"We went looking for sex traffickers, not drug dealers," said Al. "Have you found any signs of that?"

"No, but if Javelina is using the kids for bag drops, then you know she's up to other dirt. If I can get in with her, then I can find out what."

"Or maybe you can end up dead," he said. "I didn't agree to this. And I know I wandered off there for a bit. But I had the thing."

"Sure. The thing with the guy, the girl, and the *objet d'art.*"

"Right. So let's start again. Walk me through it. Who's Javelina again?"

"Ms. Roseangel Javelina, AKA Angel. She runs the Youth Center. Anyone who gets caught with an infraction gets sent to her. If I get busted with drugs, I get sent to her, and then she'll blackmail me into doing whatever it is that they're doing. I can find out how big the organization is. I can get the evidence to shut them down."

"Or maybe she'll just call the cops and you get busted for felony possession with intent to distribute."

"No, she won't."

"You're that certain?"

"Yeah, I am. Also, although I haven't actually weighed them, I'm fairly certain my... dealer cut the amounts to make sure I'm technically under felony weight." She hoped Al hadn't noticed her hesitation around *dealer*. But he didn't need to know Domingo's name and he certainly didn't need to know that Shark had approved the sale. His last brush up against Shark had made neither man happy and she'd had to pretend Shark was strictly a business acquaintance.

"I'm unhappy that you have a dealer," said Al, his fingers drumming on the table.

"Poor choice of words," said Peri. "I happen to know people who deal. I would be willing to bet that you do too."

"Not the point," he said.

Peri shrugged. "Anyway, the individual I know did not think I was being smart either, so I believe he cut the weight." Al picked up one of the bags and weighed it in his hand. "Which is fine," said Peri. "I really only need to look dirty for Angel to take me. But she'll only pick me if I have a car. All the kids doing the big errands have cars."

"I don't like this plan," said Al. "The opportunity to get arrested is high and it puts you at too much risk. You were just supposed to hang out, nose around, and figure out which one of the staff members was spotting girls for sex trafficking. This is way more than just some scumbag staff member."

"Yeah, I know," said Peri. "That's what I've been trying to tell you."

"Then we should let the cops handle it."

"Fuck you. No," said Peri. "These are the fuckers who killed Vicki, and I have spent way too long looking for them to back off now."

"Do you have any evidence of that?"

Peri was silent. The only evidence she had wasn't something she could share. "I can feel it," she said.

"If these really are the people who trafficked your friend," said Al, patiently, "then that is all the more reason to let the cops handle it."

"I have been letting the cops handle it!" Peri took a breath, trying to tamp down on the rage she felt. Al never reacted well to emotions. She had to keep a lid on it, or he'd stop helping her. "I've let them handle it for almost five years, and they have gotten exactly nowhere. Vicki was kidnapped, she was sold, and then she was shot. And if Vicki wasn't enough, then what about any of the other fifty kids that have gone missing since then? The cops have done nothing, and they don't want to do anything."

"That's not true," said Al stubbornly. "But it's a cold case and they don't have a lot to work with."

"It wasn't a cold case five years ago," snapped Peri.

"Yeah, but after the shit show that went down with Vicki and everyone in that house… That crew, whoever they were, packed up and left town. The cops tried. I've read the file. They really tried. But five years ago, the trail went cold, and it hasn't gotten any warmer."

"You read the whole file?" asked Peri, feeling a flight of butterflies in her stomach.

"Yeah, where do you think I got all those police reports in your precious book from? I copied all the relevant parts out of the file."

Peri glanced at the coffee table in the living room. Underneath it was her macabre scrapbook of missing and dead kids and all of the little bits of paper that had led her to Happy Place. Al had reluctantly helped collect them, but she hadn't realized that he'd actually put forth the effort of getting Vicki's whole file. That meant that he'd probably burned at least one of his favors at the police station.

"All the missing kids in the last year link to Happy Place," said Peri.

"It's circumstantial," argued Al, like he wasn't the one who'd found the link in the first place.

"That's why I should go in," said Peri. "If I can get names and locations and find out who's running things, then you can call the cops and say you happened across some evidence in pursuit of one of your cases. I won't even have to be involved."

Al grunted. Which meant that he was thinking about it, but he wasn't happy about it.

"I get that you're worried, but I'm being careful. I'm not about to go off on some sort of Chuck Norris one-man against an army revenge spree or anything. As soon as I've got some evidence, then we can go straight to the cops." Al tugged at his beard, but didn't say anything. "Anyway, I was thinking that if you were to buy me a car tomorrow," she pushed the pile of cash in his direction, "that I could go get caught with my drugs and we'd be in business."

"I'm not agreeing to this yet," he said. "Also, you'll need some driving lessons."

"Yeah, I've got a friend who does street races. I was going to have him show me some stuff."

"Absolutely the fuck not," said Al.

Thursday ~ March 9

Shark: The Reyes Brothers

Shark parked the car at the gas station and went inside. Unlike the suburban gas stations that he had been growing accustomed to, this one had only two parking spaces, one of which was filled with Vivian's decidedly non-departmental issue SUV. The clerk looked up from helping a customer and jerked his head toward the Employees Only door. As directed, Shark walked into the back room. Ryan Holden was with Vivian again, and she was looking even more pissed than usual. Shark had been in the city three days, and each day seemed accompanied by an angry call or text from Vivian.

"You bring me to the nicest places," said Shark, looking around.

"You said you would have direct evidence of who Geier was buying from by now," said Vivian without waiting.

"He buys from the Reyes Brothers," said Shark. "It's not a mystery."

"That doesn't do me any good," said Vivian. "I need more."

"The buy is happening tomorrow," said Shark. "After that, I can't tell you what I don't know."

"Well, find out," said Vivian. "We have a deal, and if you can't perform, then I will put you back in prison."

"Is this your version of sweet talk? I have to say it needs work," said Shark. "In case you didn't know, the Reyes brothers are extremely strict about who shows up to their meetings. I can't go unless I'm invited."

"So get invited."

Ryan was watching them with an amused expression. Shark wondered if people flipping shit at Vivian was always funny or if Ryan just hadn't seen it done before.

"I have been," said Shark. "I've been sucking up to Pompo and I'm invited."

"So where and when is the buy?"

"Tonight, sometime," said Shark with a shrug. "I don't know the location or time. But chances are all I'll be doing is hanging around by the truck. I'm not going to come back with much."

"When will you find out the location and time?" demanded Vivian.

"When Pompo tells me, after Geier tells him."

"These things take time, Viv," said Ryan, frowning. "You're pushing the kid too hard."

"He's not a kid," said Vivian, giving Ryan a disbelieving stare. "He wasn't a kid, even when he was a kid."

"I have no idea what that means," said Ryan. "But even if he gets something, we're not moving on it. We're trying to build cases, not take down scores."

Shark wanted to say *No fucking shit,* but refrained and tried to redirect.

"I can't turn it around this fast. The only way I'm moving up is if Pompo suddenly takes a powder."

"So make that happen," said Vivian.

Shark threw up his hands in frustration. "How about some help for a change?"

"Pompo Akamine?" asked Ryan. "Is that the guy we're talking about? I pulled his jacket a couple of months ago. There are a couple of angles we could—"

"You could mind your own fucking business?" snapped Vivian. "Make it happen," she told Shark, denting his chest with her French-tipped manicure before stalking out of the room.

Shark looked at Ryan, who shrugged. Shark rolled his eyes and left. He should have known better than to think Ryan was going to be helpful. Shark was at the bottom of Vivian's shit list, and Ryan wasn't going to want to join him there. Shark cruised back toward his apartment and thought about trying to do something productive. Instead, he stretched out on his fancy new bed and prepared to take a nap. He never would have thought he'd miss the basic condo of the suburbs with Marko and the guys popping in and out. His new place had all the furniture he loved and seemed twice as empty.

Two hours later, the phone rang. Shark picked up the phone and saw the unregistered number with the prefix that he'd come to associate with FBI phones. He hit the green button, expecting to hear Vivian's voice and more complaints. Instead, it was Ryan Holden.

"I arrested Pompo. We can hold him for forty-eight hours

before we have to charge him. Good luck." Ryan didn't wait for a reply; he simply hung up the phone.

Shark dialed Marko.

"What do you know about the Reyes bros?"

"Superstitious mother fuckers," Marko replied instantly.

"But what kind? Like Catholic superstitious?" Shark went to the closet and pulled down the black duffel bag that was all that remained of his pre-prison possessions.

When Shark had gone into prison, Geier's relationship with the Reyes Brothers had been fairly new. Shark wasn't sure if anything he knew about them was still relevant.

"No, they're real Indian or whatever they call Indians in South America. They're into black magic and shit."

"Anything else I should know?"

"They're suspicious as hell from what I hear. Always worried about narcs and shit. I mean, they are still here, so clearly that has paid off. But that makes them prickly to deal with. If you know what I mean."

"Yeah, I know the type. Thanks. Do me a favor, send Beef up to me ASAP. I'm going to need someone who has my back tonight."

Shark dumped the bag out onto the bed, looking for what he needed. Then he stopped, staring at the random assortment of junk on the bed. When he'd come out of prison, he'd had nothing.

He had known that's how it would be, and he tried not to care. He had no family. His mother had died in some crack den when he was seven. His father, whoever he was, might be alive somewhere, but who knew or fucking cared? And Aleja Santoyo, his grandmother, the one who had raised him, had died of a heart attack when he was eleven. There wasn't anyone in Geier's crew who gave a shit about him. He was alone, and the only possessions he had were the ones that he'd been carrying when he'd been arrested. When he'd gotten out, Vivian had shoved it all in the black duffel bag, and he hadn't opened it since that day.

Sunglasses, crucifix and Santa Muerte medal on a chain, wallet, weathered set of lock-picks, rubber-banded deck of tarot cards, and two paperbacks—a new translation of The *Book of Five Rings* by Miyamato Musashi and *Bodas de sangre* by Federico García Lorca.

He picked up the crucifix. It had been a gift from his grandmother. He remembered her telling him how to use it. How to look for the superstitious and the religious. How to listen for the things they needed to hear. She'd made him memorize all the right prayers and go to church, but she had slapped him when she caught him praying for his mother. Religion, she said, was a game of con artists, and he was to use it as a tool, but never as a crutch. The same went for the Santa Muerte medal. Rooted in the old Mexican gods and often called the patron saint of the cartels, Shark had used Santa Muerte on more than one occasion to fit in with his co-workers. The deck of tarot cards was equally useful. The lock-picks had also been a gift from his grandmother. He had been nine when she handed them over and told him everything was fair game as long as he didn't get caught. Shark looked sadly at the bed. Every item reminded him of his grandmother in some way. She had given him the tools to survive, but more importantly, she had taught him how to think.

Reluctantly, he opened the wallet and stared at the only picture inside. He was about four, sitting on his mother's lap, and his grandmother stood proudly behind them. His mother was smiling. His grandmother wasn't. But that was typical. Aleja had never liked to express emotions publicly, while Edilira had always craved them. It was the only picture of them he had left. He remembered the day CPS had come to put him in foster care. The social worker had put his clothes and belongings in a black plastic garbage bag and handed it to him. That's when he knew that if he wanted to keep anything, he had to keep it on him. To them, everything he was and had belonged in a garbage bag.

He knew the reason he hadn't wanted to open the duffle—he was ashamed. His grandmother had survived in the US with barely any English, and she had ruled their block. She had protected him and everyone else in the neighborhood. And he couldn't even get himself out of his own mess. He was ashamed that he hadn't been able to avoid prison in the first place. Ashamed that he hadn't been able to hold on to what he'd accomplished. And ashamed that he was working for the FBI.

He picked up the deck of tarot cards and dropped them in his pocket. Then he pulled the crucifix off the chain and put the Santa Muerte medal around his neck. He scooped everything else back into the bag.

It had occurred to him that had he known Marko four years ago, he might have had something left. It had also occurred to him that if he succeeded, if he got the FBI what they needed, that Marko would be the one coming out to nothing. If he came out at all. Shark was doing what he could about that—keeping his crew out of the reports he gave Vivian and keeping them isolated from Geier. But he had to worry about himself first. He didn't dare make any overt moves yet.

Shark waited until Beef arrived, and then they drove down to Kos. He watched Beef absorb the bustle of the neighborhood as they walked to the back entrance. Beef had the skills and talent to be in the city. Shark had occasionally wondered why the hipster leg-breaker had never asked to be bumped up. It wasn't until they were upstairs that Shark remembered that Beef, with his man-bun and yoga pants, stood out like a sore thumb. If Beef wanted to be in the city, he would have to adjust his style—maybe for him, that wasn't worth it. Shark spared a thought to wonder how any of his team would fare without him. Not well, he suspected.

"Hey," said Shark loudly enough for Geier to hear. "Has anyone seen Pompo?"

Devonte looked up as Shark spoke and then scanned the room as if looking for his boss. Devonte's hair was freshly shaved and sported an exotic design in the fade. Shark appreciated the artistry, but thought that it was too flashy for the environment. It was too likely to draw Geier's attention.

Everyone shook their head. They all knew Geier disliked raised voices at the restaurant. Shark pretended to check his phone and waited for Geier to call him over.

Moments later, Geier waved him over.

"Is there a problem?"

Shark pretended to hesitate. Then shrugged. "Pompo said I should go with him on the Reyes buy tonight. He wanted to meet early and finalize the details, but I haven't heard from him, and he's not picking up."

Geier looked displeased. He snapped his fingers at Devonte. "You. You're one of Pompo's. Where is he?"

Devonte approached close enough that Shark could smell nauseating waves of body spray. He'd had to mandate a maximum number of sprays for his underage crew at the bowling alley and allow free use of the bowling alley shower to prevent similar nasal assaults. He considered it his charitable contribution to mankind, not that they passed out awards for that. Devonte glanced at Shark as if for guidance, and Shark kept his face neutral. "He was going to get a massage and then meet me here for the Reyes buy." Geier looked epically unimpressed, which was enough to make Devonte nervous, and the kid backed up a few feet. Shark knew Geier liked that kind of fear—it stroked his ego—but it wasn't going to do Devonte any good if Geier really decided to hold Devonte accountable for Pompo's absence. "He should have been here a half-hour ago," added Devonte.

Geier slapped Devonte in a hard open open-handed strike.

"I do not like it when my people are late," hissed Geier.

"I'll go find him," said Devonte, backing up and trying not to trip over his own feet. No one in the room moved to help him. "He probably just got… uh, extra happy at the end of his massage and fell asleep. I'll have him back here in twenty minutes."

Shark thought the last part was a mistake. It was a promise he knew Devonte couldn't deliver on.

"Twenty minutes," said Geier, checking his watch. "That's it."

Devonte was already out the door. Geier looked from Devonte back to Shark. Shark wondered what he saw when he looked at them. He and Devonte were about the same age, about the same height, probably about the same background, but Shark didn't feel they were in the same weight class.

Geier turned to Crease. "That kid couldn't find shit in an outhouse. Make some calls, see if you can dig up Pompo. I've got a bad feeling about this." Crease nodded, took a few steps away, and began to work his phone.

"We went over it a little last night," said Shark. "I can go without him, but I'd need the location."

Geier looked thoughtful. "The Reyes brothers don't like new people. They won't be pleased with a change."

Shark shrugged. "I can back Crease then."

"They like blacks even less than new people."

Shark threw his hands up in the air, as if washing his hands of the situation.

"You know what," said Geier, a smile hovering behind his eyes. "Why not?" He pulled out his phone and texted—Shark's phone pinged seconds later with an address.

Geier went into his rarely used office and came back out with a nondescript black backpack. He tossed it over to Shark, who caught it, but didn't bother to open it and confirm the cash inside. "Tonight at six," said Geier. "Don't come back without the product."

"When do I not?" asked Shark.

"First time for everything," said Crease, sourly, looking up from his phone.

They left Kos to arrange transport. Beef waited until they were outside before speaking. "It's a fucking trap of some kind, right?"

"Yes," said Shark. "Geier thought it was too funny for it not to be."

"But why do that? I mean, we need the product, so why set you up to fail? I don't get it."

Shark shrugged. "You don't have to get it. Just don't ever forget that's who we work for."

Beef took a breath and put up a hand to feel his top knot. "Marko said I was to watch your back. I thought he meant from you know, other gangs and shit. I didn't think it would be…"

"From our own people?"

"Yeah." Beef looked embarrassed to be saying it out loud.

"I know the guys think I'm extremely rigid about not talking about our business to anyone, but this is why. The wrong word to the wrong person in that room, and we're all dead. You get what I'm saying?"

"Yeah," said Beef, nodding. "Yeah, I do."

"Good," said Shark. "Meet me at the warehouse. We'll pick up the truck and a couple of guys to load it and go from there." Beef nodded again.

"Got it."

They arrived at Geier's warehouse and went around to the loading dock, where a couple of guys were smoking cigarettes and shooting dice. They looked up as Shark and Beef approached.

"Who's on the exchange tonight?" asked Shark, looking over the crew.

"Dino, Jerome, and me," said a blocky, Latino guy stepping forward. Shark recognized him as someone he'd punched before, although he had no memory of why. Shark struggled to remember his name and eventually came up with Jesús. "Where's Pompo?" asked Jesús.

"Not coming," said Shark. "It's me tonight."

Jesús crossed himself and muttered something in Spanish before hurrying off into the dark.

"Where the hell is he going?" demanded Beef as the rest of the men began to drift off.

"Down the street to light a candle at the church," said Shark, going inside to collect the keys to the truck in the office. He and Beef would ride in the cab, while Jesús and the other two had the unenviable job of riding in the enclosed back.

"Well, that's not real fucking reassuring," said Beef.

Shark grinned.

"And also, what the fuck?" demanded Beef. "Not a lot of trust."

Shark shrugged. "No," he agreed. "That's OK, though. That just means he's smart. And I'd rather have a smart guy riding in the back."

"No," said Beef firmly. "Smart money is always on you."

Shark snorted a half-laugh. "Beef, don't place that bet. Sooner or later, my streak is going to break."

"It ain't a streak when you're good," said Beef.

"Said every gambler everywhere," said Shark drily.

"Well…" Beef's pale face split in a wide smile, "yeah."

Shark shook his head and went to inspect the truck. Tonight

was not the night to get tripped up by a busted taillight or fritzy starter.

The Reyes Brothers warehouse was on the docks, surrounded by a wood and chain link mish-mash fence and guarded by serious-looking men and even more serious dogs. Their logo, a Mayan circle with a leering face in the center, was painted on the fence with the words REYES BROTHERS SHIPPING curved around it. The air smelled of dead fish, creosote, and diesel. The blue and yellow cranes at the port loomed like mammoth skeletons outlined against the sky in the spring sunset.

They arrived at the warehouse on time. Shark was folding the tarot cards through his fingers. He had purchased the deck particularly for the size. Most tarot card decks were oversized, designed for impact and to maximize artwork. Shark had selected a standard playing card-sized deck that could fit in his pocket and would keep his skills with cards sharp.

The truck was allowed through the gate. Shark and Beef slowly and carefully exited the cab under the watchful eye of three men with AK-47s. Shark left Dino and Jerome at the truck and went in with Beef and Jesús.

They were patted down. They gave their names. And then they waited. Shark continued to shuffle the deck, remembering the feel of it.

Finally, a man wearing an open-knit top and an Uzi approached. It was so very eighties.

"You are not Pompo," he said accusingly.

Shark turned so that the Santa Muerte medal could be easily seen, and then, with his left hand, he put down the deck on a crate and pulled three cards off the top, laying them face down in a row. The man with the Uzi eyed the procedure carefully. Shark turned over the three cards, again using his left hand.

Card one was the Ace of Pentacles, card two was the Sun, and Card three was the Six of Wands.

The man looked at the cards and licked his lips. "Those are good cards," he said.

They damn well ought to be good cards. He'd spent a lot of time reading up on tarot and marking the deck. Who wouldn't want new opportunities, abundance, and cash?

"Pompo is unavailable," said Shark. "I'm Shark. I'm his replacement."

"We don't do business with new people," he said.

Shark looked down at the cards and then up again. "Are you sure?"

"Wait here," said Uzi guy and trotted off.

Beef looked like he was dying to make a comment, and Jesús looked reluctantly impressed. More time passed. Shark shuffled the cards some more and waited. Eventually, the guy with the Uzi came back.

"OK, they'll see you. This way."

They followed him towards the far wall of the warehouse, where a room had been constructed. It pulsed with music, and Shark could see and smell the pot smoke leaking out from under the door. It was going to be one of *those* kinds of transactions.

Hopefully, it didn't turn out to be one of *those* kinds of nights.

They were ushered into the room. He had the impression of being crowded, but between the smoke and layers of rugs, pillows, and blankets, it was hard to tell if the impression was accurate or not. A hookah sat in the center of the room and was being manned by two girls in gold bikinis. The Reyes brothers, twins differentiated only by shirt color, sat on the far side of the hookah on plush thrones or possibly just mounds of pillows, sharing a giant spliff. Behind him, he could hear Beef and Jesús trying to breathe through their mouths and not cough on the smoke.

"Where's Pompo?" one of the brothers demanded. Shark didn't see which one.

Shark flipped over the top card of his deck—it was Justice.

"No one has said, but…" he held up the card.

They nodded in unison. They were about forty and wore their hair long. Their indigenous heritage could be seen in the arch of their noses and smooth, ochre colored skin.

"We have heard of you," said the one in the red shirt—Rojo. "We heard you killed a man with one punch."

"It was two," said Shark, resigning himself to the fact that the story about Big Paulie was not going to die.

"We heard you went to prison for love," said the one in blue—Azul.

"It was manslaughter," said Shark. He paused to think about Francesca and the disaster of a relationship that had led up to his prison sentence. "And really hot sex."

That got a laugh. Shark realized then that he could have laughed with them, which was the first time in almost five years that had been true.

"We heard," said Rojo, "that you can do magic. That you make the impossible happen."

Shark flashed his teeth in genuine amusement. The answer to this one was easy. "Anyone can do magic," he said. "But first you must do the work."

They nodded again, again in unison—the magic of twins.

"We see why Geier sent you," said Azul. "We will do business with you. The merchandise will be loaded in your truck. You have the cash?"

Shark nodded to Beef, who stepped forward with the black backpack. Rojo waved to the Uzi flunkie, who took the bag and checked it. Uzi flunkie stood up and looked to the brothers, waiting.

"But first you will need to test the product," said Rojo. "We don't trust those who won't join us." Another gold bikini-clad woman stepped forward with a silver tray. Shark wondered if the bikini was provided as part of the job or if she had to get her own. A single line of coke had been beautifully laid out. She put it on a table next to the hookah. Everyone looked at him expectantly.

Shark shuffled the tarot cards again, more for time than anything else.

It was believed that undercover agents wouldn't do the hit. Which was ridiculous. There were also plenty of fairly straight dealers. Dealers who did too much of their own product don't last long. But this request, with the girl and the silver platter and the intense scrutiny, had the air of a ritual. He sensed that this was the last test and he'd better get it right. What had Pompo said? He got the job because he was good at doing drugs?

Beside him, Jesús was staring at him as if to beam a message into his brain. He didn't need the help. He got the memo just fine.

He shrugged. "OK." He put the cards down on the table and leaned down to do the line. It had been several years since he'd done any blow. He'd forgotten about the incredible smack of the drug against the membrane of his nose or the intense rush of energy. They had not skimped on the quality. He stood up, and his hand bumped against the deck of cards, knocking one off.

"Hold it up," said the blue twin, pointing to the card.

Shark did as he was told.

"The lovers," said Rojo.

"Gemini," said Azul. The brothers exchanged pleased looks and nodded.

And, like that, the meeting was over. Shark, Beef, and Jesús were ushered back to their truck. Jesús clapped Shark on the shoulder with a grin and went to help load the truck.

They got in, and Beef took the wheel.

"What the fuck just happened?" demanded Beef. "Did we just pull that shit off based on some fucking tarot cards and a line of coke?"

"Something like that," said Shark, trying to fight the smile off his face.

"But you don't even believe in that shit!"

"I don't have to, as long as they do," said Shark. The coke was buzzing his brain. Coke, to him, was a masculine drug. Not because only men could do it, but because it stoked the ego and made him feel powerful. Drugs like E and acid were feminine.

They made him feel more empathetic and connected. On a basic level, one caused more punching, the other caused more hugs.

Right now, it was making him want to get to the warehouse and deliver the shit, so he could rub it in Crease's face.

They were halfway back to Geier's warehouse when Shark saw the street light start to drip in shades of yellow.

"Uh, Beef," said Shark.

"Yeah?"

"When we get to the warehouse, we unload and then we bug out, OK? We're not going inside, and we're not going to chat with anyone. In fact, if you can, keep people from talking to me at all."

"OK, why?"

"Because I think I just did a pretty heavy hit of acid along with that line of coke."

"Shit. Uh… OK. Can you maintain until we unload, or should I drop you off somewhere?"

"I've got to maintain until we unload," said Shark. "I've got to be seen bringing it in, otherwise this little exercise was for nothing. I can make it until then. But after that, take me back to my place in the 'burbs and call Marko."

At least with Marko, he'd be safe.

Peregrine: The Dessert Factor

"I can't believe we had to come all the way out here," said Emma as they went back to the car. "I'm going to be so fucking late if I run you home."

Emma started to tear up, and Peri sighed. She wasn't sure how much longer she could take guard-dogging Emma on Javelina's errands, let alone listening to Emma's *problems*. Getting a *B-* in Pre-Calc was a reason to get a tutor, not a life-threatening emergency. A life-threatening emergency was the fact that after delivering another bag full of drugs to another drug stash house, their odds of getting tetanus or MRSA had just quadrupled. Not that Emma had noticed. She'd *ewwwed* over their mark's totally uncool jeans, but hadn't noticed the open sore on his arm. Peri couldn't decide if it was some sort of self-protective denial or if she really was that clueless.

"I mean, really, I'm going to be grounded for a week!" Emma gave a dramatic sniff. "I don't understand why my life has to be so hard!"

Peri tried to keep her eye roll low-key, but thought she was only partially successful. It wasn't like she didn't have other things to do. Between school and Emma, she'd barely managed to squeeze in her own errand to her personal pot dealer—a hippy named Matilda who was possibly still wanted on a 1974 warrant for environmental terrorism. The things Matilda didn't know about pot could be written on a Post-it note. She baked a variety of personalized edibles to assist with medical problems. Peri's was insomnia. She'd been making a lot of trips to Matilda recently. Matilda had said she was worried. That meant Peri would have to see a different dealer next time.

"I just think that no one really understands how hard it is to be me," said Rachel. Peri turned away so Emma wouldn't see her expression. She looked down the street—a strip mall with restaurants cast an alluring glow.

"Tell you what," Peri said, "Why don't you go straight home? I'll catch a Lyft."

"Are you sure?" asked Emma, already getting in the car.

"Yup, not a problem." Emma was away before Peri had finished her sentence. Peri shook her head and walked toward the strip mall. She checked in with Otto first, only to discover he was booked solid for the next hour, and then checked the reviews on the restaurants in the strip mall. She was seriously considering moving to plan B on the car front if Al didn't come through with a car soon. She had other cash, and she knew people who knew people at chop shops. Getting a car shouldn't be this hard. Her restaurant choices were Ethiopian or Mexican, and she settled on Ethiopian after a quick skim of the reviews. The restaurant had almost universally high reviews, except from the one jackass who complained about having too many ice cubes in his water. There was always that one jackass.

She walked through the door of the restaurant, scanned the interior, and stopped as she locked eyes with Marko. They stared at each other, trying to assess next steps. Finally, he shrugged and waved her over. She dropped into the chair across from him. There was more staring.

"I know you didn't follow me," he said.

"I didn't even know I was coming here," she said.

"Sheer coincidence?" he asked.

"That's what I'm going with," she said.

"I haven't ordered yet," he said. "You want something?"

"I just want dinner," said Peri with a shrug. "Whatever you want is fine with me."

"Getting off work?" he asked.

"Yeah," she said, and he laughed at her expression.

"Must be an exciting gig."

"Too many fucking junkies," she said.

Marko grunted his understanding. "You must run your shit, not let your shit run you. Other than that, you doing OK?"

"Same old, same old," she said. She looked around the restaurant. "I've never been here before. What's good?"

"Don't know. I haven't been here either. I was just going to order a little of everything. In the city, it's so easy. You just hit every restaurant in the neighborhood or wait for the menu ninjas to slide something under the door. Out here, everything is so spread out. I have to look up what places to go to. Nobody delivers shit, and they all fucking close at ten. How am I supposed to get food at two in the morning?"

"I usually either hit the hospital cafeteria or the grocery store."

"The hospital! I hadn't thought of that."

"You wouldn't like it," said Peri. "A lot of cops go there, too. They all think I have a sick aunt, but I think you'd probably find that harder to pull off."

Marko grunted his agreement. "You know the other weird thing about the suburban restaurants," said Marko, looking around, "is the space. I mean, look at this place. You could legally get at least three more tables in here. They're not maximizing the floor at all. They're losing money. Of course, in the city, they'd probably have six extra tables and a friendly fire marshal on speed dial."

Peri laughed and relaxed down into the booth. It was nice to be with someone who didn't require any pretense.

"Hey," she sat up, suddenly remembering a question that Marko was qualified to answer, "Now that I've got you here…" She hesitated. Maybe it was rude to ask? Marko's face showed a careful neutrality that meant he was worried about what she was going to say. "What do you know about crepes?"

His face relaxed into his usual smile. "They're a thin pancake of French origin that can hold a variety of toppings."

"Yes, thank you, genius. What do you know about making crepes? I'm part of a group project on France. I volunteered to make crepes because I figured it was easier than writing shit. But I tried to make some last weekend and now I'm thinking I should have fucking done the writing."

Marko laughed. "They're harder than they look. And of course you're going to get better results with a better pan."

By the time they were done with dinner, she felt ready to take on crepes a second time. She was also in a far better mood.

Marko had not mentioned Shark once and instinctively seemed to know not to ask about anything overly personal. That should have left them without a topic of conversation, but instead, they had ranged across a wide variety of matters from current affairs to the history of the noodle.

"I don't know if I should spring for the pan," she said as they walked out.

"I think you're going to be a lot happier," he said. "Give you a ride?"

She debated saying no, then shrugged. "Why not?"

Marko's Cadillac was always plushy to ride in. He was religious about detailing, and she worried some about tracking in dirt, but she liked rolling like a mob wife every once in a while.

They were still debating pans in the car when Marko's phone began to ping with texts. He grabbed for the phone and unlocked it as they were pulling onto the freeway. He managed to unlock it on a quick fumble, but the lean of the car tossed it from his hand and into her leg space. She grabbed it and felt her mouth go dry and her heart rate speed up.

"It's Beef," she said, picking up the phone. "He says…"

"He says what?" asked Marko, looking over at her, a crease forming between his eyebrows.

"He says to go to Shark's place, now. There's a problem with the boss."

She felt the car pick up speed. "I can drop you off," he said.

"Just go," said Peri.

Beef, his long hair swinging down around his shoulders, answered the door with relief and barely blinked at Peri. She slithered around him and looked around the condo. It looked the same as ever, no blood or disarray, but it was slightly cold and musty, as if the heat hadn't been turned on in a day or two.

"What's the problem?" demanded Marko, coming in and surveying the interior as Peri had. "Where's Shark?"

"He's in the bathroom. I can't get him out," said Beef.

"I'm sorry, what?"

"I went up to the city, like he said. We went to pick up the shipment from the Reyes brothers," continued Beef. "But he's new, so they made him do a line. At least, it might have been because he's new. It might have been because they're fucking weird."

"OK, so? I mean, I know Shark doesn't use much these days, but it's hardly his first bump. What's the problem?"

"They laced it with acid," said Beef. "It kicked in a couple of hours ago, but we had to deliver the shit and then come back here." Marko looked as if he wanted to ask a question. "He told me to bring him back here instead of his place in the city." Peri digested that information. Shark had always been headed out of the suburbs, but it still stung that she hadn't known he was already gone.

"He said it was safer. But now I can't get him out of the bathroom. He keeps fucking throwing bars of soap at me."

"How much soap can be in the bathroom?" demanded Marko, walking to the bathroom in the master bedroom.

"More than you'd think."

Marko looked inside and then immediately ducked back as a bar of soap came hurtling through the doorway. Peri walked past Marko and stood in the doorway of the bathroom.

Shark was sitting on the floor and leaning against the glass wall of the shower. Next to him was a decorative basket full of soap. He was staring at the ceiling. She walked in and sat down on the toilet, letting her backpack slide down to the floor. She really hadn't thought the first time she would see him again would be in a bathroom while he was tripping on acid. She thought about opening the shower door and turning on the cold water because she felt like he'd at least earned that one.

He pulled his gaze off the ceiling and looked around the room, finally focusing on her.

"You're not really here," he said.

"I'm not?"

"No, that would be nice. And nice never happens to me." And then he smiled at her, and that was enough to break her resolution for revenge. "The ceiling's not really breathing either," he said as if telling her a secret.

"Well, that's good," she said. "I'd be worried about that."

"I burned our picture," he said, leaning forward. "And I regret it every day."

Peri raised an eyebrow. As far as she knew, they had never taken any pictures together. She didn't know how to respond to that one. "We can take a new one?" she suggested.

He was now focused on the garbage can.

"How about we go sit in the bedroom?" she asked, hoping to move the focus back to her.

"We have to protect the soap," he said.

"From what?" she asked.

"From Beef. Fucker keeps trying to steal my soap."

"He does smell too clean," she said, and he laughed.

"I hate this shit," he said, leaning back against the shower door again. "It makes my brain lie to me, and it makes me tell the truth to everyone else."

"And we can't have that," she said.

"No, we cannot," he said, sounding for a moment like sane Shark.

"I'm going to talk to Marko for a minute," said Peri. "Don't go anywhere."

"Good idea. I'll stick with the soap."

She went back out to the bedroom.

"Get anywhere?" asked Marko.

"Well, number one, who the fuck has an entire basket of soap?"

"It's one of Geier's places," said Marko. "I think he had his staging company decorate it."

"Whatever. Anyway, there appears to be a need to protect the soap from Beef. I think if Beef weren't around I could probably talk him into going to lie down on the bed."

From the bathroom, they heard Shark moving around.

"I can go chill in the living room," said Beef. "I'd be a hell of a lot happier if nothing else."

"That's the shit," said Shark from the bathroom.

Marko exchanged looks with Peri, and they all tiptoed to the bathroom door.

"Oh, son of a bitch," said Peri. "Not the entire damn thing!"

Shark paused, with half her brownie in his mouth. "It called to me," he said, pointing to the open side pocket of her backpack.

"Sorry about your dessert," said Marko.

"That's not dessert," said Peri. "That's a medicinal pot brownie for insomnia."

"So he's done coke, acid, and now pot?" asked Beef. "He is going to be *so* hungover. At least he doesn't have to worry about peeing in a cup."

Peri let that comment slide by. "OK, everyone out. I'll see if I can get him in bed before he passes out."

She went back in and sat on the toilet. He finished off the brownie, crumpled up the cellophane, and chucked it overhand into the sink. He looked around and saw her, which made him smile all over again.

"I really wish you were here," he said. She knelt down next to him and put her hand up to his cheek. "Oh Jesus," he said and turned his face into her palm.

"Come on, let's go into the bedroom." She boosted him to his feet, and he went where she pushed him. He stumbled into the bedroom and flopped down face-first onto the bed. She poked his side until he rolled over.

"Fucking Geier," he mumbled, as she managed to capture one of his feet. "I knew this was going to suck."

She tossed his shoes toward the closet. "You knew it was laced?"

"I knew it would be something."

"Why the fuck did you take it?"

"Had to," he said. "They wouldn't have completed the sale otherwise."

She pushed on his feet and legs until he crawled into the center of the bed.

"Cotton feels like purple," he said, staring at the ceiling.

She sat down on the edge of the bed and leaned over him. His pupils were enormous, but his breathing seemed fine. She leaned back against the pillows and took a moment to check her phone for messages and consider what to do next. She hadn't come to any conclusions when he rolled over and draped an arm and a leg over her, snuggling his face into her shoulder and breast. She sighed and reluctantly put her arms around him. She knew she shouldn't let him touch her, but her body completely disagreed with her brain on that subject. She ought to have walked out the second she'd seen he was fine. But he smelled good—like lemongrass and soap. And he'd been so happy to see her. And damn it, she wanted to. She let herself enjoy the feeling of him pressed against her just for a moment. She watched as his eyelids slowly drifted closed.

"Are you sleeping with Vivian Flood?" she asked.

He didn't move, didn't even tense up.

"It seemed like the best solution at the time," he said.

"I'm sure that it did," she said.

"Don't be mad at me."

She sighed. "Not right now," she said, kissing the top of his head. "I'll be mad at you later."

"As long as there's a later," he said. He turned his face into her and inhaled. "I miss the way you smell. I miss your skin. I miss how I get buzzed when you're around. I miss the way you tell people to fuck off." His words trailed off into a slur, and his eyes closed. She waited five more minutes, allowing herself to enjoy the weight and heat of him, and then rolled him off of her. She took his face in both her hands and kissed him.

"I miss your stupid face," she said.

She tucked a blanket around him and went back out to the living room.

"He's going to be hungover as fuck," she said. "You guys might want to get him some green tea and dark chocolate. Make sure he eats something when he wakes up. And I always recommend a nice walk or some light working out, but I doubt you can talk him into that."

"What are you, my fucking dealer?" asked Beef. "I thought drugs weren't your scene."

"A significant portion of my income comes from kids who did the wrong fucking combo. Why do you think I don't do shit? Anyway, Marko, can you still drive me home, or should I get a car?"

"No, I'll drive," said Marko with a sigh.

The trip to her house was silent. Peri couldn't come up with anything to say that wouldn't sound like a slightly less whiny version of Emma. Why hadn't he called her? If seeing her was so nice, then why wasn't she curled up in bed with him right now? If he missed her so much, why was she locked out of his life? She knew he had his own secrets—she got that—it went with his job. It's not like she told him everything about her shit. But then she never told anyone everything. She kept everything carefully segmented, blocked, and compartmentalized. Mom, school, Al,

Trey, Vicki... Nobody knew everything. But Shark was the only person she'd ever felt like she *might* be able to tell everything to.

"Thanks for your help," said Marko, as he pulled up at her house. "Do we owe you anything?"

"I swear to God, Marko, if you reach for your wallet, I will shank you."

"Wouldn't dream of it," he said, smiling. Then he sighed. "I don't know why you two can't work out whatever it is that went wrong."

"Maybe you should ask Shark that question," she said.

Marko snorted. "I don't want to get punched to death."

"Well, then maybe you should leave it alone," she said.

"Probably true," he said, sighing again. "See you around, Peri."

"See ya, Marko," she said and slammed the door.

Friday ~ March 10

Peregrine: The Day After

"Mm-hm," said Peri, as she unlaced her shoes. Regan, captain of the drill team, could yap for an unbelievably long period of time without actual input. Drill team practice had been somewhat of a disaster. They were insisting that Peri could not sit out the game this time. Between Shark and an impending public performance, she had lost all ability to think.

"Oh my God, Peri, for reals, can you focus?" Regan snapped her fingers in front of Peri's face. "What is up with you? You have been zoned out for, like, the entire practice."

Peri looked at the blonde and weighed her options. Regan flaunted her curvaceous figure with a confident swagger that Peri envied, and more than that, she had a cut-throat approach to sex and relationships that resonated with Peri. Regan appeared to feel zero guilt about putting her own needs first in any relationship—if someone wasn't meeting her standards, she moved on, and boys could go cry somewhere else if they had a problem with it. Maybe Regan would be able to help Peri get things straightened out in her head. She could not be this off her game by the time she got to Happy Place, which meant some emergency head cleaning.

"I found out this guy I like slept with somebody else," said Peri.

"OK," said Regan. "Number one, who is this guy? Because finally! Trey has been out-of-state for, like, ever. I was starting to think you were turning bi. Or whatever Madison calls it because she can't hack that she's a lesbian. Number two, when you say *slept with*, what are we talking about? Like, did he get oral at a party one time or did he do the nasty with some skank?"

"It's just this guy. And I thought he didn't like me. And then I found out that he does like me, but he slept with, and might still be sleeping with, the skank. Who, to be fair, is pretty hot."

"Meh," said Regan. "I've seen you in the locker room. You can compete."

"Thanks. Anyway, now I don't know what to do. We weren't ever together really." Regan was giving her skeptical face. "We made out a few times," she said by way of clarification. "So you know, it seems like I can't be mad at him because that wouldn't be fair."

"What does fair have to do with it? Fucker led you on. You can be mad at whoever you want to be. This is the heart, you know? The heart feels what the heart feels. I say roll with mad and move on to payback."

"OK, yeah, so I'm kind of mad, but also…" Peri trailed off, suddenly embarrassed to say it out loud.

"But you're still kind of into him?"

"He's just so…cute," said Peri, settling for a juvenile turn of phrase. Everything else seemed too personal and *just so Shark* would be meaningless. She flung her gym shoes into her bag and pulled out her Converse high-tops.

"That's where the bastards get you," agreed Regan, nodding. "What you need is to find an appropriate level of payback, and then if he grovels and ditches the skank, I say go for it."

"Appropriate level of payback is hard," said Peri.

"Show up with someone else. Let him feel the pain."

Peri laughed as she pulled on her sweatshirt. She actually couldn't think of anyone who could possibly make Shark jealous. There wasn't anyone who could compete with him.

"I mean, you still have Trey. Unless your relationship status has changed?"

Peri shook her head. Nothing had changed between her and Trey. At least on Trey's side of the equation. Trey was great. Trey was perfect. But she wasn't what Trey loved. Trey loved the version of Peri that had stopped existing almost five years ago. That girl wasn't coming back, and pretending to be her was getting more and more difficult.

"You naughty girl," said Regan, looking impressed. "I did not think you had stone cold cheater in you."

Peri sighed. "It's not cheating."

"Oh, it's not? Did mystery boy have his hands on your boobs?"

"Well, I mean... yeah. But..."

"But, what?"

Peri stared at Regan, trying to formulate an answer. But... Trey was better off in California without her. What she barely wanted to think, and had added to the list of things she could never say, was that *she* was better off with Trey in California. The problem was that she didn't want that to be true.

"Trey is… he's moving on to a new life. He's in a new state. He's going to be going to Stanford. And it's not like I don't love him. I do. But I'm not going to be there for that life. I can't keep pretending that I am."

"Well, then break up with him."

"Absolutely not," Peri blurted out. "His mom just died. He's living in a whole new state. How am I supposed to be like, *peace out*? He needs me."

Regan looked skeptical. "So what he doesn't know won't hurt him?"

Peri shrugged. "I'll add it to the list." Keeping secrets barely registered on her guilt-o-meter anymore. Regan nodded, but still looked thoughtful.

"All right. Well, to return to the problem at hand and focus on mystery boy, I say have Trey call you while you're with the other guy and then be all cutesy."

Peri tried this plan out in her head. She didn't think Shark would be jealous of Trey. Shark was the only person who knew what she'd done for Trey. He would understand why she couldn't just dump Trey. Wouldn't he?

"I will think about it," said Peri, because that was the polite thing to say about advice.

"You need a ride home?" asked Regan, zipping up her bag.

"No, my uncle texted that he was going to pick me up." Peri

checked her phone to confirm that her uncle had indeed sent such a message. It was unusual, and that made her suspicious.

"He's the one who teaches you the kung fu maga or whatever?" Peri snorted at Regan's mish-mash of martial arts. "Did I tell you that Raizy used that move you showed us on Nolan Mathews in the lunch room?"

"What? Really? Where was I?"

"It was your Running Start day," said Regan, with a shrug. "He tried to pick her up and dump her in the trash can, and she went for it. Did the yell and the elbow in the stomach and everything."

"That is so awesome! Why does Nolan think that's funny? He is such a dipshit."

"It got a round of applause," said Regan proudly, as they walked out of the gym. "Wow," she said, staring at Peri's uncle, who was parked in a fire lane, standing next to a car and checking his phone. "Your uncle drives the lamest car ever."

Peri looked at the boxy, older model beige-gray-ugly-colored Volvo and felt her heart sink. "Actually, I think that's about to be my car."

"Well, at least you won't need to worry about birth control. That car radiates more disapproval than my mother. You are so never getting laid in that thing."

"I'm guessing that is exactly what my uncle was going for," said Peri. Regan laughed. "Hey, Al," said Peri, coming down the stairs. "Nice parking."

"Thanks. So what do you think? Is this the new Peri mobile?"

"It *so* is," said Regan. "It really just screams Peri. I think you should name it Chastity."

Al switched his focus to Regan in surprise. "She's funny."

"A laugh riot," said Peri, while Regan grinned unrepentantly.

"Well, Chastity is fully air-bag equipped, has new tires, a good set of brakes, and has had a full check-up. She's good to go."

Al beamed proudly at the car. Peri took a deep breath and reminded herself that the car was a means to an end, that boring meant less likely to be noticed, and that Al was showing his love through safety. But she couldn't help thinking that Shark would be horrified.

"It's great, Al, thanks," she said with a smile.

He looked at her suspiciously. "There's nothing else you want to say?"

"Nope. It's great. Thank you for helping me out."

He looked disgusted. "It's no fun if you just say thanks."

"It's an ugly fucking car, Al," she said.

"Thank you! Was that so hard?"

"You two must be a delight at Thanksgiving," said Regan.

"Just don't touch the pumpkin pie and everyone gets out alive," said Peri.

"I'll keep that in mind," said Regan with a laugh. "All right, I'm out. Good luck with Chastity. Nice to meet you, Al. See you tomorrow, Peri!" Regan waved as she headed for her car.

"She's funny," repeated Al.

"Yes," Peri said. "Because when I bother to hang out with people, they are usually bright and intelligent. Stop sounding so surprised."

Al shrugged. "So sue me. I expect teenagers to sound like their brains have been used for snacks by aliens."

Peri rolled her eyes. "Never mind your somewhat rational prejudices. Come show me how this thing works."

Three hours later, Peri felt that her driving skills had taken a significant leap forward. Perhaps teenage car thieves and drag racers didn't make for the best driving instructors after all. Considering that Al had been training her to fight since she was thirteen, she shouldn't have been surprised that he was a good instructor, but somehow the change of venue still made it a shock.

"What are you going to tell your mom?" asked Al as she dropped him off.

"That you bought me a car and you're teaching me to drive."

"I wish you wouldn't involve me in these things," he said.

"It's a bit late for that," said Peri.

"No kidding. You're really set on doing this?"

"Yes."

"Ok, well, from now on, I want texts every time you enter and exit that place. And tell me where you're going any time you do work for them."

Peri nodded. "Will do. I'm starting tonight. I told everyone yesterday I was getting a car."

Al sighed. "How do I let you talk me into these things?"

"It's a mystery," said Peri. She didn't correct his misapprehension. She never talked Al into anything. She simply did what she wanted until he couldn't resist the momentum of events or he felt the need to provide a safety net. He grumbled the entire time, of course, but he was reliable as a clock. Or, she suspected, as her new Volvo.

Peregrine: Happy Place

The Happy Place Youth Center was located in a suburban industrial park, surrounded by printing firms, auto-body shops, a software firm, and a slushee supply company. The building was a concrete block painted beige. The only thing really attractive about it, from a teen point of view, was that it was easily accessed by several bus lines.

Peri parked and went into Happy Place with an unusual feeling of nervousness. She wondered if this was how everyone else felt when they tried *not* to get caught. She checked her knife out of habit, feeling the smooth, flat crest of the knife blade folded flat into the matte black handle. She had a couple of different knives, but this one was her favorite. The grip was the right amount of texture to prevent slippage. The weight felt nice in her hand, and it was slim enough that it tucked into almost any pocket discreetly, although she almost always wore them in an elastic belt around her waist under her shirt.

This late in the day, the center was mostly empty. A handful of Javelina's *special kids* mingled with the staff. The *specials* were low-esteem, socially awkward little puzzle pieces who generally were looking desperately for approval and a hint of love. It made them the perfect targets for Javelina's exploitation.

The interior had been subdivided into so-called fun zones.

There was a climbing wall, an obstacle course, a darkened laser tag zone that mostly kids just made out in, a computer lab for homework, and a cafeteria-style dining area. Javelina's office was in the back, near the kitchen, and had a window in it that had been silvered like a two-way mirror so that she could watch the activity in the lunch room without being seen herself.

Peri passed the laser tag area where, from the muffled moans emanating from the other side of the door, a pair of someones were using the space for a little more than making out, and went into the dining area. Someone had decorated it in drooping dollar-store shamrock garlands pinned to the walls. Peri tried to pick out which of the waste-of-space employees had bothered. They didn't seem like the celebrating the holidays crowd.

At a table, Ken, one of the counselors, was ostensibly offering homework help to one of the girls, but as she watched, Ken's hand dropped onto the girl's thigh. Ken was a dark-haired jerk-off in his late twenties with a permanent leer and a tattoo of an ex-girlfriend on one bicep that protruded from below the sleeve of his Happy Place polo shirt. He hadn't bothered to cover her with another tattoo. He'd simply had someone tattoo X's over her eyes. But the most damning to Peri was the tattoo on the other forearm—a strange symbol in all black, shaped a bit like a Q. A lot of the staff had them. When questioned, the staff members just laughed and said it was sort of a symbol for Happy Place.

Peri walked over and put her bag down on the table in front of Ken. She had strategically placed her red diamonds in an unzipped pocket of her bag, but no amount of bag waving seemed to catch his notice. His hard-on was visible through his pants.

The girl was sinking silently in on herself and trying to lean away. Peri tried speaking directly to him.

"Hi Ken," she picked up her bag, "do you know where Ms. Javelina is? Is she in her office?" She looked around, pivoting to display the bag. "Or at the gym?" Pivot again.

The girl took the opportunity to gather her things and run.

"I don't know where Angel is," he said, looking annoyed at Peri's continued streak of interrupting his attempts at molestation. He looked around as if expecting the director of the youth center to appear and totally missed the drugs in Peri's bag. "Why don't you go find her?"

"Maybe you could show me where she is?" suggested Peri. She knew he wasn't going to want to get up with the tent pole in his pants, but she wanted him to feel embarrassed. He glared at her, and she waited.

"No, I'm fine here. You go find her."

"Feeling OK?" she asked, faking concern. "Should I get someone? Hey, everyone—" Peri raised her voice to draw attention to Ken.

"She's in her office!" he barked, interrupting.

"Thanks," said Peri. "You might want to do something about that stiffy, by the way. You look like a pervert."

She walked toward the office, trying to formulate a plan. She didn't actually have a reason to talk to Javelina. She had been counting on Ken not being quite the mouth-breather that he was. Her head was down as she considered her options and tried to look like a depressed teen when she heard the distinct light tap of high heels on industrial carpet. This was her opportunity.

There was an art form to tripping convincingly. Peri wasn't sure she nailed it totally, but it was close enough. When she looked up from her sprawled position on the floor, the red diamond baggies had spilled out in an arc in front of her. Peri looked further up and saw Roseangel Javelina.

Directors of teen programs, in Peri's experience, tended to be a frumpy mom or dad type with a terminal case of caring. They could never figure out how to dress appropriately because they were too busy to go shopping, too likely to spend their money on their cause, and too tired to care what they looked like.

To Peri, Ms. Javelina always looked like she was wearing a costume. While the rest of the counselors drooped around in polos and khakis, Javelina's slacks were tailored, and her shirts freshly pressed and styled with flipped cuffs, pearls, and sweaters. Somewhere north of forty, medium height and curvaceous, with dark hair in glossy spiral curls, Javelina wore the uniform, but somehow still managed to look like she was about to go yachting instead of to the lunch room. No one else seemed to notice. In fact, Peri had heard envious sighs from the other girls. It never occurred to them that it was only possible to look that put together if you had enough free time to devote to skin care and shopping. A youth center director should barely have time to think, and Javelina had a fresh manicure every two weeks.

"Well," said Ms. Javelina, squatting down and picking up one of the red diamond bags, "we don't see many of these around here. And you have, oh my, five."

"That one has always been a trouble-maker," said Ken, from behind her. "I think we should call the cops."

Peri looked over her shoulder. Ken had found a jacket and he was holding it in front of himself. She looked back at Javelina, trying to look panicked. Remembering to emote was her weak point.

"I was holding them for a friend," Peri said.

"Of course, you were dear," said the director. "But I think you're going to need to come into my office to discuss this." She looked around and spotted Emma by the office door. "You'll wait here with Ken, while I discuss some things with Emma. And remember, dear, if you run, we will call the police."

Peri looked at Ken. He looked smug. Peri tried to look cowed.

"Emma dear," said Javelina, "let's talk for a moment."

Emma looked at Peri, her expression worried, but followed the director. The door was shut for a few minutes, and Emma came out, tucking a baggie full of red pills into her pocket. Javelina beckoned to Peri, but before she could enter the office, a cell phone in the director's pocket began to ring. Javelina checked the number and then made a wait gesture to Peri and Emma. Ken rolled his eyes and began to check his phone.

"Don't worry," said Emma, in a near whisper. "I told Angel you were cool."

"Are you going to Tommy's again this week?" asked Peri.

"Don't know," said Emma. "I told Angel that I didn't want to go there again, and she said not to worry about it." Emma looked around and leaned closer. "I heard that Tommy lost a shipment a few weeks ago. I think they're still pissed at him. So hopefully I won't have to go back out there at all."

Peri raised a skeptical eyebrow. "If he lost an entire shipment, how are they still working together?" What she meant was: *how was Tommy still alive*, but she didn't want to freak Emma out.

"I don't know. I guess he got it back. Anyway, I told Angel I'd take you out and show you the ropes. She doesn't know you've been going with me already." Emma giggled at their secret. "But hopefully that means she'll give us something easy this week."

"Sounds good," said Peri with a shrug.

"Oh, there's Ally and Carissa. They're graduating this year, you know. Guess that means they won't have to hang out here anymore."

Peri glanced at the other two girls who had just come in. Neither one went to her high school, so she relaxed.

"I hear Ally has a route that tips her. I wonder if she could put in a good word for me. I could use the extra cash."

Emma buzzed away, and Peri edged closer to the office door.

"I don't know," said Javelina, sounding dubious. "They're not as reliable—" Whoever was on the other end cut her off. "Well, that's a point," said Javelina, sounding more convinced by the other speaker's argument. "No, I've got reserves. I can send some tonight. It's more about delivery. Give me a few hours to figure it out. Yeah, OK, I'll call you later."

She hung up the phone and waved Peri in. Peri used the confusion of collecting her bag to hide hitting record on her phone.

"I just talked to Emma," said Javelina. "She seemed to think very highly of you."

Peri smiled with real nervous energy. She hoped Emma hadn't overdone it. "She's pretty cool," said Peri.

"You're sixteen now? Didn't I hear you saying you were getting your license and a car last week?"

Peri nodded. She'd put herself down a couple of years when she filled out the paperwork. She'd wanted to fit the profile of sex trafficked kids.

"This friend of yours that gave you these, did he happen to mention that if you get caught with them that it's a felony?"

"Felony?" wavered Peri.

"Yes, that's prison time," said Javelina.

Sure, if you ignore the fact that Peri was a juvenile, white, first-time offender, with a good lawyer. Not to mention the fact that once Javelina had confiscated the drugs, the police didn't actually have any direct evidence that Peri had possessed the drugs in question.

"Oh God!" said Peri, wishing she could squeeze out some tears. "But I'm a good person!"

"Of course you are! But you see what a problem this presents me with. It's not like I want to call the police. I'd rather not have them within ten feet of any of my kids. And that's how I feel—that you're my kids. I want you to think about me like a mother."

Sure. The Greek Tragedy kind of mother who killed her own children.

"But, but," Peri pinched the soft flesh on the inside of her arm and managed to tear up. "Please don't send me to prison. Please, Ms. Javelina!"

Javelina appeared to consider, trying to make Peri sweat.

"You should probably call me Angel," she said. "Because I think maybe, this once, I can answer your prayers." Peri wondered how often she used that line. "But if I help you, I would expect you to help me."

"Anything!" Peri widened her eyes to their fullest.

"It wouldn't be hard. I just need someone to run errands for me."

"I could do that!" exclaimed Peri eagerly. "Just please don't call the cops!"

"Well, you'd have to help out for a while," said Angel with a smug smile. "And this would just be between us. I don't want other kids thinking they can get away with things or that I'm a pushover. But I can tell you're one of the special ones—like your friend Emma. I think you deserve a second chance."

"I won't tell anyone!" Peri wondered if the classic heart cross was too juvenile, but it seemed in character, so she went for it anyway. If anything, it made Angel smile wider. The woman came around the desk and sat in the chair next to Peri.

"You know, Peri, I know this little arrangement is unusual, but I only do it for the kids I really care about. And I want you to feel like you can tell me anything."

Peri was impressed with the way Angel looked truly caring. Was it the wide eyes? The soft smile? She had to figure out how to copy that.

"So if you have any feelings, special feelings, about Emma, I want you to know that's OK."

Peri blinked. What was going on? She'd been distracted by analyzing Angel's expression and had forgotten to track the actual content of her words. "I... uh... don't really know," Peri mumbled and dropped her voice to near silence. That always played well in the teenager genre.

"Because we welcome everyone here," said Angel sincerely, and she put her hand on Peri's shoulder. Peri resisted the urge to bat it away. "And we really celebrate all kinds of love. Some kids like to take pictures, you know, and we think that's beautiful. Or if you're really not sure, but you just want to experiment? We can create a safe place for you to really explore your more mature side. Because I can tell that you're a really smart girl. Too smart to be caught up in any sort of what's right or wrong, black and white view of things. I'm right, aren't I?"

"Well, I am pretty smart," said Peri, watching Angel with horrified astonishment. Angel had jumped straight to child porn. Shouldn't there have been more grooming? Heck, she really expected wine and flowers if nothing else. "But I don't know about taking pictures or anything."

"Of course not," said Angel, backing off slightly. "I just want you to know that you can trust us here. I want you to know what your options are."

Assuming that her options were child porn, then sure.

"Right," said Peri. "Thanks."

"Did you want to spend some more time with Emma?" asked Angel with a conspiratorial smile.

"Yes, please," said Peri, trying for eager.

"I think I can arrange it. We'll start you with something easy early next week." Outside the office, they both heard Ally's distinctive snorting laugh. "Is that Ally and Carissa?" asked Angel, leaning over to look through the doorway.

"Yeah, they just walked in," said Peri.

"Great," said Angel. "I think we're done here, don't you, Peri? We understand each other, don't we?"

"Yeah, I think so," said Peri, shyly.

"I'm so glad. I can tell we're just going to be the best of friends. Can you go out and send Ally, Carissa, and Emma in? I think I have a special errand for them tonight."

"Tonight?" repeated Peri.

"Don't worry. They're really mature and experienced. They know what they're doing. I won't make you go with them."

"Oh, OK."

"Now shoo, and send me the other girls."

Peri went out and did as she was told. "Call me when you're out," she hissed to Emma as they passed her. Emma nodded mutely.

Shark: The Warehouse

Shark walked down the corridor of high shelving toward the center open area of the warehouse. He could see Geier, Crease, and a handful of the favorites already waiting. He prepped himself, preparing to be energetic and bold. He felt nothing close to either of those things. Whatever fucking combo he'd done had delivered up the best night's sleep he'd had in months. The dreams had been fucking bizarre and mostly full of Peri, but he felt ridiculously relaxed. What he really wanted was coffee, a couch, and a newspaper that he could pretend to read while taking a nap, but that wasn't going to do much for his reputation.

"You son of a bitch," said Shark, striding forward and going directly to the drinks cart. There wasn't quite a gasp, but he felt a collective intake of breath from the room. "You knew, didn't you?" he asked, turning toward Geier, gesturing broadly with his empty glass.

"Knew what?" asked Geier, his face the picture of innocence.

"You knew about the lucy in the coke!" Shark tossed ice cubes into the glass—they made hard, emphatic plinks against the glass.

Geier began to laugh.

"I'm so glad my fear and paranoia can amuse you," said Shark, filling the glass and shaking his head.

"It does! It really does," laughed Geier. "They do it to every-one new, or they don't deal. It's not like you could have gotten out of it."

"The fucking ceiling was breathing, man! You could have warned me!"

Geier laughed harder. "Where would be the fun in that? Come on—don't tell me you're really mad. You didn't enjoy it just a little? You're always so uptight. You needed to loosen up a little."

That was Geier—he liked to put people in a position where they had to agree with him or fight. Shark rolled over and let him win. That was how the game was played.

"Meh," said Shark, as he flopped down on a dove gray suede Noguchi knock-off love seat and stretched out his legs. "It was more the surprise of it. After that, it was fine."

"It must have gone well," said Geier. "They called this morning and said you are now their preferred liaison."

Shark paused with the glass halfway to his mouth, startled and aware that the room was watching him. "I thought it went well. I didn't think it went that well."

"They said something about auspicious symbols?"

"Possibly. To tell the truth, the evening is a little fuzzy," he half-lied. The last thing he needed was Geier figuring out that he had arranged to take over Pompo's position.

No, we can't have that.

Peri's voice was crystal clear and loud enough for him to look to his left on the couch. He'd done enough LSD to know a flashback when he felt it, but all of his previous flashbacks had been to something he at least vaguely remembered. This time was like having a vision. Shark deliberately took a drink and tried to stop himself from sweating. Had he seen her? Had she been there last night? Why didn't he remember?

Geier was speaking again. He'd already missed part of it.

"—cements our supply line. But I have called you all here to discuss our problem: the goddamn Scarecrow Jack."

A twenty-something youth with the pasty complexion of someone who spent too much time with his computer and a joystick wheeled a large screen TV out into the meeting area. He began to tap at a laptop, and pictures appeared on screen. Shark realized that Geier now had his own AV guy.

"Last week we were hit at three locations." The AV nerd, a pale, lanky kid who looked to be sweating buckets even in the cool air of the warehouse, showed photos of the three houses while Geier narrated. "We lost all product and cash." A spreadsheet of lost profit. "Not to mention the street-level head-bashing that's been going around. We're losing ground and I'm fucking tired of it."

The AV kid rested the screen on a map showing dots where every incident had occurred.

"And do we even know who this guy is? No, we do not. So we are going to work this fucking problem. I want suggestions and I want them now."

The AV guy flipped to a clip art of a light bulb.

"Go back," said Shark. "Go back to the map."

The kid looked nervously at Geier, clearly uncertain if he was allowed to take direction from others.

"Yeah, go back," said Geier. "Shark hasn't been around. Let

him see what real territories have been dealing with." Acquiescence and a dig at him at the same time. Geier was a fucking judo master of assholery. "Now let's hear from the group."

There was chatter that Shark ignored. The street-level dealers didn't concern him. The stash houses did. Two of the locations were ones he'd given Vivian to keep her out of his hair. That made him nervous. The third was a new location he hadn't known about, which made him feel slightly better. He got up and went to stand closer to the screen. Each dot had a date next to it. The stash houses had all been hit on the same day. He turned to the AV nerd.

"Do you have casualty statistics?"

"Casualty rate is 100%," said the nerd, blinking. He had dark, floppy hair, and he flipped it out of his eyes like a horse batting away flies. Shark tried not to laugh in his face. It was such a teen heartthrob look. No guy ever counted on the fact that they'd be flipping their hair like a girl when their hair reached a certain length—they just thought long hair looked cool and rebellious. Then came the desire for headbands.

"And all the bodies were accounted for?"

"Yes," said Crease, sounding annoyed. "They were. Nobody went conveniently missing."

"What about times?" asked Shark, ignoring Crease.

"I've got a time overlay. Hold on." A minute later, the map appeared to blink, and times had been added to all the dots.

"Is there something you would care to share with the class?" asked Geier, holding up his hand for silence. The territory bosses shut their mouths and turned to Shark.

"What do your Federal snitches say about this?" asked Shark.

"Not a damn thing. There's some sort of Internal Affairs push. Everyone is clammed up. Why?"

"Because it feels Federal," said Shark. "The disparate locations—"

"Disparate?" repeated Crease sarcastically.

"It's a vocabulary word meaning distinct and unlike one another," said Shark. "Look it up. The disparate locations with the simultaneous timing? That feels…"

"Like cops," agreed Crease. "But it can't be. There would be arrests, not deaths. There would be press releases and shouting about winning the war on drugs."

"I agree," said Shark, "But that makes me wonder if—"

"If Scarecrow Jack has better snitches than we do?" asked Geier.

"Maybe. It doesn't have to be, I suppose," said Shark. "It could be that they just have some people with training. Ex-army or something."

Geier audibly chewed through an ice cube from his whiskey glass. "I want to hit them."

"We can't," said Shark.

"Not yet," said Crease at the same time.

Geier glared at them. "Are your cycles syncing up over there? Why the hell not?"

Shark glanced at Crease and retreated to the couch. Technically, this was Crease's arena.

"We don't know enough. Onesie twosie stuff—it won't

amount to much. It won't make a big enough dent. We need to do to them what they did to us. We need to hit them all at once."

Geier glanced at Shark, who nodded.

"So you're advising me to do nothing? Gentlemen, I don't think you're getting the urgency of the situation."

Shark and Crease exchanged looks. "We get it," said Shark. "But we don't have enough information. We need to figure out their supply line. Figure out who the major players are and take them out."

Another ice cube was destroyed while Geier mulled over his options.

"I've been looking into the hardware they used to hit us," said Crease. "Some of it was unusual and probably from Shark's Agent Fowler. I've got a line on some people who sell that shit. If I can find out who sold it, I can find out who bought it and who used it."

Shark tried not to look aggravated that Crease had a plan already moving. So much for hitting the ground running.

"OK, here's what we're going to do. Crease, you're running point. Go break whatever heads you have to. Chase your hardware. Meanwhile, Shark, I want you to collect some of the younger guys, go hit the streets and the clubs. Find me dealers, find me whoever has a name. I want heads by next week."

Shark: Emblem Night Club

Shark sat at the table and felt a growing sense of frustration. He couldn't believe Geier had pushed him into going along with the junior league. Devonte, Malone, and their contingent of gang-bros were his age, but he felt like the fucking babysitter. They couldn't focus, didn't understand simple directives, and every other word out of their mouths made him want to start punching and not stop until they shut the fuck up. And now he was in a velvet-rope blocked table by himself while his five so-called contemporaries had evaporated into the crowd. Shark shook his head. It wasn't that he didn't like clubbing. He'd been clubbing since he was fourteen. It was fun. If you liked who you were with. Or if you weren't worried about someone slipping you some *E* and then saying the wrong thing. But that wasn't why they were here. They were here to do a fucking job, and those jackasses were out trying to get laid.

He grabbed his jacket and prepared to leave, but found himself stopped stone cold as Peri walked by. Or danced by, to be more accurate. God, she could move. She was dolled up in a pair of Lycra pants and some sort of punk t-shirt top thing that, he was willing to bet, concealed her knives. She was wearing high heels, which was unusual for her. It was Peregrine Hays company policy to only wear shoes she could run in. On the other hand, movement in those shoes did not look like a problem. She was trailed by some idiot with slicked back hair and leather pants. She stopped at the bar and waited to catch the bartender's eye, continuing to sway to the beat.

The meathead in the leather pants pushed his way in next to her. Instead of rebuffing him, she looked amused. Shark walked over and leaned into his ear.

"Beat it."

Meathead looked offended. "I was here first, man."

Shark stared at him and watched the boy wilt down. Meathead looked at Peri for support, but she looked even more amused and shook her head.

Shark stared at her, and she stared back. Unlike most people, she never had a problem making eye contact. Now that he was here, he didn't know what to say.

"Buy me a drink?" she suggested.

He wanted to counter with something cool, but really, he had nothing, so he did as he was told. He signaled the bartender and leaned over to yell his order.

"Vodka shot and a cherry Coke. Put it on table eight."

The bartender nodded, but with a disgusted look. He put the shot down in front of Peri and the Coke in front of Shark. Shark took the shot, and Peri reached for the Coke. He downed it and set the glass down and watched the bartender's expression change. Then he realized that the disgusted look hadn't been for ordering soda, it had been for staying sober while getting a girl drunk.

"I have a table," said Shark, pointing toward the VIP section.

The music wasn't as loud here, but he still had to speak at an almost yell to be heard. She shook her head and pointed at the bar-height table a little ways away. He shook his head and she shook hers again, then grabbed his hand and headed toward the table, dancing as she went. Their progress was interrupted by other couples making their way to or from the bar, and as a result, he repeatedly found himself with armfuls of Peri as she bounced to the rhythm. He breathed in her scent and tried not to think about her naked.

They finally made it to the table, and she set down her drink and turned around toward him, but he became aware that her gaze was fixed on a table off to his left. He stifled his disappointment.

"You're working?" he asked, leaning in so he could speak at a normal tone into her ear. She nodded and moved closer, still dancing. "Those guys?" he asked, glancing over briefly at another VIP table. There were three guys and a flock of women around. They looked like douchebags. The girls looked uncomfortable and tense and held their oversized purses in front of themselves like shields.

"Those girls," she corrected, as her hip bumped against his leg. "I'm here to make sure the three miniskirts make it home tonight."

He wasn't sure what the rules of this game were, but he was enjoying it. He knew he should ask her about the previous evening. He should talk to her about her uncle. He ought to say a lot of things, but he didn't want to. He wanted to enjoy this moment of Peri dancing close to him, body brushing up against his.

"And what are you going to do if something happens?" he asked into her ear. She smelled like a flower he couldn't place.

"Very bad things," she said. She did a quick spin and slithered against him. He was finding it hard to concentrate. He reached for her, but she stepped away and took a sip of her soda.

"Why did they come if they thought bad things would happen?" he asked. He was unwilling to let her get away that easily, and he pulled her into him by the hips. There was resistance in her frame, but he ignored it, daring her to speak. She set down her drink and gave in, relaxing against him. She continued to bounce a little but leaned against his chest, tilting her face up to speak in his ear.

"Little birdies in the mouth of a crocodile sometimes get nervous." She clicked her teeth together in a snapping bite. The sound of her teeth made him squeeze reflexively tighter on her hips. He slid his hand up a few inches, under her shirt, feeling the smooth softness of her skin and the edge of her knife belt.

"Shouldn't be with crocodiles," he said and nibbled her earlobe.

"Don't have a choice," she said as she exhaled. Then she stepped back and shook her finger at him.

OK, rule one: touching, but no participating.

"Who are the guys?" he asked, moving closer again.

She reached back for her drink. "I thought you might know," she said, playing with her straw.

He looked again. They didn't look familiar. He shook his head. "Why?"

"Same line of work," she said, with a shrug.

"Not our guys," he said. But now he was wondering whose guys they were.

"Convenient for me. What are you doing here?" she asked, stepping closer again. "Working?"

"When am I not working?" he replied, pushing a curl out of her face. Her hair was thick, and he loved the heavy feeling of it in his fingers. He always wanted to bury his hands in it.

"I don't know," she said.

"Peri," he began, still not sure what to say, but wanting to say something.

She leaned in, kissing him, her teeth raking his bottom lip as she pulled back.

Rule two: no talking about anything serious.

"You are killing me," he said, forgetting anything but the way her body felt against his, and the sweet, sugary taste of her lips.

"Good," she said, stepping back. "OK, gotta go," she said. "Thanks for the Coke." He stood in shock for a second, then turned to watch her go.

She was following the three girls across the floor at a safe distance. They were being escorted by one of the douchebags and walking quickly, no rhythm, backs tense toward the hallway. He wavered for a moment between anger and indecision, then gave up and went after her.

The hallway between the dance floors was quiet. Quieter anyway. The bass beat of conflicting songs made for a contrasting, reverberating heartbeat. There were couches scattered along the walls, occupied by couples talking or making out, and a steady stream of people going to and from the coat check near the door. Peri was following the three miniskirts as they headed for the coat check station. He jogged to catch up with her.

"Hey!" he said, too loudly for her taste because she stopped immediately, ducking behind a column, her face flashing anger.

"Do you mind? I'm working."

"Yes, I mind! What the hell was that in there?"

She checked the status of the girls and then looked back at him.

"Payback," she said.

"Payback for what? Peri, I don't turn on a dime. You need to give me something to work with."

"You don't..." She trailed off, seemingly unable to complete a sentence. "I told you I would be mad later, didn't I?"

He felt a dull tingle of dread and *déjà vu*.

"Well, welcome to later," she said and punched him in the stomach. He doubled over, breathing through his nose. His girl did not hit like a featherweight. She made as if to storm off, but then realized that the girls were still in line at the coat check.

"Didn't think that one through, did you?" he gasped.

"Fuck you," she said, folding her arms over her chest, distancing herself from him as much as possible without actually relocating. He leaned against the wall and took a few deep breaths.

"When did you tell me you'd be mad at me later?"

Her expression suggested he drop dead.

"OK, that means it was last night because that's the night I can't remember. What did I say to you, Peri?"

"Memory problems? Really?"

"I'm not faking! I had coke, acid, and apparently a pot brownie."

"Yeah! My pot brownie!"

"I'm lucky I remember anything from this week. What did I say to you?"

Her eyes narrowed as if considering. "You told me that you slept with Vivian Flood."

Shark felt a cold wave of relief, followed by a fresh wave of fear. "Ah," he said, probing his memory, hoping for a spark of recognition. What else had he said?

"Ah? That's it? I should have punched you twice."

He fought the urge to back up.

"In my defense, you and I weren't together at the time."

The expression on her face suggested that perhaps he should have given in to the desire to back up. "Who gives a shit about when? You slept with her! And then you ghosted!"

Shark felt himself sweating. He didn't remember the last time he'd been so uncertain about what to say or do. He couldn't address the ghosting, and sticking to the topic of Vivian was a disaster. He went for deflection.

"Well, then I should probably tell you that I have slept with other people in the past."

"Of course you have! You're a normal human being!"

"I'm so confused," he said, as she snuck another look at the girls. Abruptly, she spun around and kissed him again. He knew it was a fake. He knew the girls were walking by, and he was only camouflage. Somehow, the message didn't quite make it to his lips. He kissed her like it was his last chance because it damn well might be. For a moment, he melted into the taste of her, losing himself to physical sensation. When she pulled back, her eyes were wide and full of hurt.

"You're confused? Try being me," she said.

She started back down the hallway, but he reached out and grabbed her wrist.

"Text me. So I know you get home."

He thought for a moment she would tell him to go fuck himself, but instead she simply pulled her arm free and kept walking.

He waited until they were all clear of the hallway, touching his thumb to his other fingers. They tingled like he was high. He took a deep breath and tried to refocus and shake the Peri buzz. Then he approached the coat check. He skipped the line and went directly behind the desk. A hundred bribed the coat check girl to show him what the mini-skirts had checked in. Three purses on one ticket. Each full of bags of black hearts.

Shark went back to the table and found Malone making out with some girl with pink hair.

"Hey," he said, kicking his leg.

"What?" Malone was annoyed.

"Across the floor. Third table from the left. You know those guys?"

Malone squinted through the strobing lights. "No. Should I?"

Shark didn't bother to answer, instead going back to the bar. He flagged the bartender.

"Another Coke?" asked the bartender, looking amused.

"Information," said Shark, holding out a fifty.

"I don't know her name," said the bartender without taking the bill.

Shark grinned. "I do. Not worried about that. Those guys, third table from the left. They regulars?"

The bartender looked. "I've seen them before, but not regulars. OK tippers. But douchebags."

"Know any names?"

"Just what's on the card for the table. Want me to pull it?" Shark nodded, and the bartender went back to the till. A few minutes later, he returned. "Jason Dawson. Even sounds like a douchebag."

Shark grinned. "Thanks."

"Hey," said Devonte, walking up. "I made a circuit of the other dance floors. I didn't come up with anything. What about you?"

Shark weighed his desire to play nice with others. It was minimal, but on the other hand, between prison and the suburbs, he had been way out of the scene for way too long. Devonte might have information he didn't.

"Guy named Jason Dawson—third table from the left," said Shark, nodding in the general direction. "He's dealing real weight. Ever seen him before?"

Devonte squinted. "No? Maybe? Give me a minute. I know the cocktail waitress. I'll see if I can get her to take a picture. I can show it to some of the guys who hang out here more."

Shark watched as Devonte tipped the waitress a hundred to take the picture. It was a decent move. Fifteen minutes later, they were standing out front for a chance to speak without being overheard or having to yell.

"It'll take some time to hear back," said Devonte, hitting send on another text. "It's, like, prime club hour, so." He finished the sentence with a shrug. "What do you want to do? Should we make a move on them when they come out of the club?"

"No," said Shark, shaking his head. "Small fish don't do us any good. We need to leave them in the water."

"So we go back in and keep an eye on them?" suggested Devonte hopefully.

"Sure, if you want to," said Shark.

"You were hooking up with someone earlier, right? I saw you in the bar with some ten in spray-on pants. Don't tell me you don't want to go find her. We should go back in."

Shark didn't move. Devonte was grinning, clearly not meaning anything by it, simply trying to persuade the babysitter to loosen up.

"She had to bounce."

Devonte looked skeptical. "OK, I mean, whatever, but I got the remedy for that FYI."

"What?"

"I got some Mexican Valium," said Devonte, patting his pocket, and Shark almost punched him on principle.

"Roofies aren't really my thing," said Shark. "Plus, I got digits." He waved his phone as evidence.

Devonte shrugged. "Whatevs. Play the long game if you want. I don't like to look that thirsty. You coming back in?"

"No," said Shark. "You go ahead. Call me if they do any-thing weird."

"Yeah, will do," said Devonte halfway through the door. "Good luck with Miss Digits."

Shark drove back to his apartment the long way. It was the quiet time of night when people were still in the theater or the club, and the traffic was minimal. He rolled down the window and inhaled the breeze coming off the river with the faint salt smell that said the tide was in. He pushed the car, enjoying the heavy torque of the engine as it accelerated around a corner and leapt into a straightaway. It felt good to be back in the city. The suburbs had a lot of cruise-worthy streets, but three times as many cops with tickets to give out. He was pretty sure he'd paid about half a cop's salary in the time he'd been in the 'burbs. In the city, as long as he didn't hit anyone, no one gave a shit how fast he was going.

He zigged around a set of cones and a public utility truck, then avoided a lumbering cement truck. The city, as usual, was rolling forward, cannibalizing and rebuilding itself. When he'd lived here before, he hadn't noticed the constant ebb and flow of teardown and growth, but now everywhere he looked, something was missing, and some new building was going up. It all seemed startling—new makeup on a familiar face. He loved the change and resented it at the same time. He felt robbed by his four years in prison. It had distanced him from his old life. Which had been the goal of getting a degree and doing all the classes and fucking therapy sessions they'd mandated. Had he known he was going to end up snitching, he would have skipped group and read more books. He'd never wanted this life—it had just seemed like the life he could achieve with the hand he'd been dealt—but he missed the ease of existence that it had brought. Everything was so much simpler when the only questions were life or death. Long term strategy required more energy.

He finally arrived back at his apartment, checking the thread he'd left pasted across the hinge with a little saliva. Theoretically, the building had a doorman and keypad elevator entry that should prevent anyone from getting into the building, but Shark could think of at least three ways in that didn't even involve hitting anyone. If he actually moved to violence or theft, then the possibilities were nearly endless. And he didn't like being surprised. The thread was in place. Everything inside was undisturbed. He stifled the slight feeling of disappointment at that. He was used to Marko or some of the guys rattling through at some point in the evening, or Domingo coming by to steal his beer and do homework. And with the scent of Peri still on his skin, he couldn't help wondering what it would be like to have someone to come home to.

He went inside, stripping out of his clothes and flopped on the bed with a Jack and Coke and his laptop.

As usual, Facebook was a fountain of information. Devonte's informants might come up with something useful, but the internet was frequently faster. Jason Dawson, Vic Solomon, and Erik Hodges appeared to do nothing more than take selfies, work out, and check in at juice bars. They were college dropouts with no discernable source of income, and they were all wearing the latest Nikes and low-end Piaget wrist watches. The question was:

where were they getting their cash, and who were they working for? The obvious answer was Scarecrow Jack. But what about the girls? The three mini-skirts, as Peri called them, had not looked particularly happy to be dropping off product, and she'd said they didn't have a choice.

His phone finally beeped. The message was a single word: HOME.

He typed in a message. Deleted it. Typed in another. Deleted it. Finally, he just typed in a heart emoji and hit send.

She didn't reply.

Saturday ~ March 11

Peregrine: The Green Sweater

By seven, Peri was tired of staring at the ceiling, so she got up. Ally, Carissa, and Emma were all sound asleep. The trip to Emblem had been silent and tense, but the trip back, just when Peri had wanted to think and consider things, had been triumphantly chatty with multiple stops to get the right mix of fast food. Once back at Emma's, they had wanted to talk about the nightclub and how awesome it had been—glossing over their fear and convincing themselves that they had been badasses. Peri had rolled herself up in Emma's old Pokémon sleeping bag, pretending to sleep, and tried to ignore them. She'd thought about just going home, but her mom had been so excited that Peri was doing something as girly and normal as a sleepover that Peri didn't want to blow it. She'd dozed off sometime around four, but by six, she was awake again. Peri went down to the kitchen. Emma's mom, Mrs. Johnson, looked up from pouring a cup of coffee with surprise.

"Did I wake you up?"

"I don't sleep well in new spaces," said Peri. Or at all.

"Did you want something to eat? There's cereal and juice, or if you wait a little bit, I can cook."

"Oh, no. Cereal will be great." Peri helped herself to the cereal, wondering how long was appropriate to wait before leaving.

"Did you girls have fun last night?" asked Mrs. Johnson.

Peri blinked, trying to remember what they had told Emma's parents. "Yes," she said. "The study group went really well. We had a little trouble getting through some of the practice tests, but Emma pointed out that some of the questions were based on the old models, so I think we should be OK."

"Was Lara there?" asked Mrs. Johnson, and Peri felt her hand tighten around the milk carton.

"Lara?"

"Yes, Lara used to hang out with Emma all the time, but I think they must have had a falling out because she hasn't been around these last few weeks."

Peri debated telling Mrs. Johnson the truth, but that would make it awkward for Emma. Currently, Emma and the other Javelina girls were Peri's primary source of information. She couldn't afford to have Emma pissed at her.

"Sorry to hear that," said Peri. "No, she wasn't there."

"That's too bad. Do you think you'll see her at Happy Place? She left her sweater here a few weeks ago. I keep bothering Emma to return it, but she keeps forgetting."

"I'll take it to her," said Peri.

"Thanks!" Mrs. Johnson disappeared into a laundry area and returned with a green sweater, cut like a hoodie with pockets and a front zipper. She folded it and put it down next to Peri.

Mrs. Johnson checked her phone, and Peri concentrated on her cereal. Not talking was fine with her. Most adults didn't have much that was interesting to say anyway. Or maybe that was just parents? Did having children kill brain cells? The child-free adults she knew seemed to have personalities. What happened post-childbirth that turned them stupid? She surreptitiously watched Mrs. Johnson trying to decide if there were hidden depths to her.

Mrs. Johnson looked up and smiled awkwardly. "Yes?"

"I was just wondering how you and Mr. Johnson met," said Peri, grasping at the first thing that came to mind.

Mrs. Johnson laughed. "I went back to Korea because my grandmother wanted to arrange my marriage."

Peri blinked and glanced at the rotating digital photo frame that showed Emma's very white father. Mrs. Johnson laughed.

"No, Roy wasn't one of them. Grandmother introduced me to several young men, and the last one… Oh my. I tried. I really did, but he was not, well, not what I was looking for. I left halfway through dinner, but I didn't want to go home to my family and tell them that. So I went to a bar and bumped into Roy. He was there on a business trip."

"Hm," said Peri, intrigued by the idea of an arranged marriage and also by the concept of a buttoned-up Mrs. Johnson at a bar.

"Are you dating anyone?" asked Mrs. Johnson. "Emma always claims that everyone she knows is allowed to date. So far in my informal poll, I would say that only fifty percent of her friends are dating."

It was Peri's turn to laugh. "I had, have, a boyfriend. His mom died last October, and he had to move to California to live with his cousins. I would say your fifty percent is probably accurate. There's probably more that are permitted to date, but honestly, as a population, we seem fairly incompetent at it."

"Well, it seems like there aren't any rules anymore, and that means that no one is allowed to complain when they get treated poorly? I don't understand it. And then the news makes it sound like sexting is rampant."

Peri nodded. "A lot of kids do that. I don't. Potential for revenge porn is too high."

Mrs. Johnson looked aghast. "That's just so horrible. How does anyone think that it's a good idea?"

Peri pursed her lips, looking for words that would help Mrs. Johnson understand. "Everyone likes feeling sexy."

"You're children," said Mrs. Johnson. "You don't feel sexy."

"Hm. Yes, that's what my Uncle Al says, too. Let me put it this way. Everyone likes feeling attractive and loved, right? Kids or not. And it's fun having a little secret. And it's not such a big deal if it's just your bra."

Mrs. Johnson's face showed dawning horror.

"And with a webcam or a phone, it's really easy. And the very second you do it, someone says, *you're so pretty*. No barriers from thought to action, instant positive reinforcement, and a large amount of peer pressure—bam, sexting."

"I suddenly want to take Emma's phone away," said Mrs. Johnson.

"She doesn't do that," said Peri, not adding that Emma was

too embarrassed by her boobs and too busy delivering drugs to bother with sexting.

"Thank you for telling me that," said Mrs. Johnson, looking relieved.

Peri took her bowl to the sink and rinsed it off. "I think I'm just going to take off," said Peri. "I don't think the other girls are going to wake up for a while, and you probably don't need me taking up space in your kitchen."

"Oh, no, you're welcome to stay, dear."

Peri demurred and took Lara's sweater upstairs with her to finish getting dressed. If nothing else, she'd prefer to avoid having to talk to Emma's friends anymore. The other Javelina girls were more similar to Emma than to Lara. Weight obsessed, logic impaired, and fearful of appearing to be other than normal, and chattering like parakeets. It had taken a great deal of willpower not to start smacking them every time they used the word *like*. Lara had been funny and smart. Not smart enough to get herself out of trouble, but at least she'd had a spine. She might have grown into something if she'd lived past sixteen.

Peri pulled her hair into a braid and decided to skip the rest of the getting dressed routine in favor of getting out of the house. She grabbed her bag, pulled on her shoes and Lara's sweater, and headed out to the car.

She started Chastity's engine and cranked the heat. She left the winding cul-de-sac of Emma's neighborhood behind and pointed herself more or less toward home. Once on the freeway, she tried to decide where to go. Arriving home at such an early hour might cause questions from her mother. Going to Uncle

Al's might cause fewer questions, and she might be able to grab a nap. It depended on Al's mood.

She knew she was starting to chafe at the constraints of being someone's dependent. Even six months ago, it hadn't seemed so hard to use the bus, or have to hide all of the assets in her room. She wasn't sure what to do about that. Trey was pressuring her to go to a California college, and she'd caved enough to send out the applications. Her mom was pushing for in-state colleges because she was under the impression that she was paying for it. Al just got the deer in the headlights look every time the topic came up. But college wasn't really going to solve her problems.

A dorm was just another version of her mother's house. It was becoming increasingly clear that she needed some place of her own. She'd done the math—she could afford her own apartment if she went with in-state tuition. She'd have to explain it to her mother with some sort of made-up job, but it could still work. And assuming she kept up her current extra-curricular hobbies, she wouldn't have to dip into any of her retirement accounts.

Somehow, she'd always assumed that if she caught the people who had tried to traffic Vicki that she would retire. But the closer she got to that, the more unlikely she thought the idea was. What was she supposed to do with her free time? Learn to knit? What did normal people do? How were they not endlessly bored?

She supposed it was possible to manage out-of-state tuition if she moved in with Trey. But if she was honest with herself, she didn't really want to. Moving in would almost certainly mean that sooner or later she'd have to tell him about her affinity for sharp, pointy objects and violent problem-solving techniques. It would also mean having sex. Which was a subject that was pressing on her mind lately.

What she hadn't bothered to mention to Mrs. Johnson was that lately, Trey had been hinting that sexting might be fun. The Peregrine Hays company policy on sexting was entirely *no,* and he hadn't come up with any arguments that changed her mind. Then there was the invitation to visit him for her birthday. And that also certainly meant sex.

Which shouldn't have been a problem. They'd had sex. And sex with Trey had always been... fine. It was just that she hadn't recognized how uninspiring fine could be until she met Shark.

Shark might run hot and cold, and he might be a mother fucking mystery, but he was not fine. Unless she meant fiiiiiiiine.

She knew that sooner or later that she was going to have to suggest to Trey that perhaps they should see other people, but every time she thought about that, her brain seemed to shut down.

She needed Trey.

She didn't need him to do much more than to always be his dimply, cheerful, supportive self, but she still needed him. Life without Trey seemed impossible.

Meanwhile, what she wanted was Shark. Seeing him last night had been a shock. She wasn't sure what had inspired her to exact her pound of flesh in the form of a vertical lap dance, but in the light of morning, it did not seem like one of her better plans. Partially because she had come away feeling like Shark had ended up with the upper hand. Being that close to him had only made her miss him more.

She pulled up at a stoplight, and she found herself pulling up the text messages on her phone. The last text sent was Shark's. Just a heart. What the fuck was she supposed to do with that? When she was with him, it was perfectly clear that he wanted her. And then it was like once she walked out of the room, she was out of sight, out of mind.

She pulled up at her uncle's and saw with relief that he wasn't home. That meant she might catch a few hours shut-eye without anyone pestering her.

Climbing the stairs to her uncle's apartment, she turned over her problems in her mind again. Shark, Trey, college. Did any of it really matter compared to Lara's lifeless eyes staring at the rain? She dropped onto the couch and pulled the blanket off the back, and wrapped it around herself. Lying down, she felt a pointy object poke her from the pocket of Lara's green sweater. Reaching into the pocket, she took out a folded piece of paper.

She recognized it instantly. It was one of Mr. Eastmire's horrible quizzes. She noted that the date was the day Lara had died. She tossed the paper on the coffee table and pulled the blanket over her head.

The next thing she remembered was a shuddering jolt of the couch moving and her knife flicking open in her hand. She blinked and looked around. She was standing up and facing Al and didn't remember how she'd gotten there.

"You're running a little hot there, Peri," he said, eyeing her sternly.

She looked around and checked the microwave, clock—it was nearly noon. She'd scored about four hours of sleep. Which, these days, was pretty good. She folded her knife back up and put it away before sitting back down on the couch and running her hand over her hair and, as an afterthought, checked to make sure her braid was in place and covering the scar behind her ear. The last thing she needed was to have *that* conversation with Al.

She looked around again. Nothing seemed out of place. "Did you kick the couch?"

"Bumped into it," he said. "Probably for the best. I don't like getting stabbed."

She grunted, which was what Al usually did to her in these situations.

"Jesus, you look like Chris when you wake up."

She stared at him, unable to process that statement. She had never thought she looked particularly like her father. Maybe in the eyes, but most people said she looked like her mother.

"You want some eggs? I'm going to make eggs."

"OK," said Peri. She looked up at her father's flag on the mantelpiece. Her mother had given it to Al. She hadn't wanted it, which had only cemented Al's opinion of her mother. Peri saw her point in some ways—what good was a flag going to do her? Her mother preferred photos of him.

"Do I really look like him?" she asked.

Al put the pan down, almost turned around, and then turned back to the stove.

"Yeah, he used to do the same thing with his hair. Same dopey look of confusion. He never tried to stab me, though."

"Pretty sure he punched you at least once," she said.

"He was drunk those times. Or I was drunk. One of the two."

"I could be drunk."

"You'd better not be."

Peri was staring at the folded paper on the coffee table. It had landed partially unfolded. She could see Lara's handwriting in bold block letters on the inside of the paper, partially covering the printed material.

"I said, you'd better not be," said Al, stepping away from the stove, spatula held at a menacing angle. She blinked up at him, trying to remember what they had been talking about.

"I don't really drink, Uncle Al. Don't like the taste."

"Keep it that way," he said, emphasizing his words with the spatula. She nodded, but that didn't seem to make him any happier.

She picked up the quiz and reluctantly opened it.

Tommy's 3 pm.

"I think I'll skip the eggs, Uncle Al," she said. "I'll just head home."

"No," he said. "No, stay. I'm just… forget about it. Ignore me. Just stay."

She stared at Al. She wasn't sure what to do. He'd never told her to stay before. Usually, he tried to push her out the door. She looked down at the note in her hand, then back up at Al. He was frowning at the eggs. He looked sadder than usual.

"OK," she said. "I'll stay."

Shark: The Other Place

Shark checked Instagram again. Jason, Vic, and Erik had split up for the evening. Erik was the only one announcing his plans on social media—a rave on the west side.

Shark exhaled in exasperation and rolled his head around, trying to stretch out his neck muscles. Really, a rave? He was feeling far too old for this shit. Who did he know that was stupid enough to do his legwork?

He dialed Devonte.

"Dude, 'sup." Devonte sounded surprised.

"Hey, there's a rave tonight on the west side."

"Yeah. You wanna go? Some chicks I know are gonna go. They're usually good for at least a BJ if you give them the right incentive."

Shark rubbed the scar on his eyebrow and tried to ignore everything that he'd just heard. "No, I'm good. But do you know any of our guys who are going?"

"A few. Why?"

"Those guys at Emblem, did you send the picture to any of the ones that are going?"

"Um, yeah, I guess."

"I want to know if any of them are selling Scarecrow black hearts at the rave."

"What should we do if they are?"

"Nothing. I just want to know if I'm right."

"Cool. I guess. Yeah."

Shark hung up and looked at his computer again. He'd been all over social media digging into Peri's drug dealers. His best lead was Cheyenne, an angry ex-girlfriend whose non-deleted posts indicated that she might have information worth learning. She had already checked into The Other Place Bar & Grill and posted two duck-lipped selfies from the women's room.

He pulled on a jacket and a more expensive watch and checked himself in the mirror. At least a bar would be better than a rave. Less glitter and getting poked in the eye with angel wings, if nothing else.

Thirty minutes later, he was leaning across the rolled metal bar top of The Other Place to yell his order to the bartender, then he turned and tapped the girl to his right on the shoulder.

"Hey, you're Cheyenne, right?"

She turned around and gave him the once-over. Apparently, he passed inspection because she smiled.

"Yes, I am. I'm sorry, I don't remember where we know each other from."

"We met at one of Jason's things," said Shark vaguely.

Her face suffused with rage. "I don't hang out with him anymore," she said stiffly and prepared to turn back around.

"Good call. That guy is kind of a douchebag," said Shark, shaking his head. "Can I buy you a drink?"

She smiled. "I'd like that. But I was about to go out on the patio…" She left the suggestion that he could come with her unspoken.

"Oh, thank God," said Shark, faking a smile. "Another smoker. I was starting to feel like the only one."

He paid for their drinks and walked her out to the patio. She was smoking an e-cigarette. He stopped at the machine and bought a real pack.

"Mmm," she said, inhaling as he lit up. "I know these things are so much better for me, but I miss the smell of real cigarettes. Reminds me of my dad."

Yay, daddy issues.

The conversation bounced around the basic getting to know you stuff. Her stories were predictable. Her flirting was predictable. Her cleavage, if he'd had an advanced degree in mathematics, was probably predictable. Mostly he thought it just wiggled like a better kind of Jell-O.

As she kept talking, he found himself comparing her to Peri. She was a few years older, and yet she seemed in many ways strangely younger. Or maybe less experienced? That couldn't be it, because having had the occasional window into Peri's jam-packed schedule, he knew that she couldn't possibly have the free time to do enough clubbing or dating to be considered experienced.

Finally, Cheyenne mentioned Jason in passing, and once more her face flushed with anger.

"What happened with that guy?" asked Shark. "I mean, I never really liked him, but what happened with you two?"

"Well," said Cheyenne, "it all started at Tommy's house."

"Tommy's the one with the green electric car?" asked Shark, picking a descriptor at random.

"No, Tommy's the one who lives up in Pomona Heights. Blonde guy? Always having parties. Has a pool. It's cool. He's kind of, like, a little too into the scene, if you know what I mean, but it was cool."

"Oh, right, Tommy," said Shark and mimed shooting up, hoping that he'd picked the right drug.

"Right! Anyway, so Jason and his loser friends always buy their shit from him, and I would go along because it was fun. So we're there and I go in the bathroom to uh... freshen up."

Yay, coke head.

"And I come out of the bathroom, and I hear Tommy talking to Jason, and he's offering Jason cash to have me go off with that creepy real estate guy."

Shark frowned, trying to picture who she was talking about.

"The bus stop guy, you know? Preston something. I'd run into him before, and he would always try and sort of pet me. But I figured he was harmless. I mean, he had a lot of money and he always gave out lots of party favors, so I figured he was OK."

Yay, standards of a guinea pig.

Shark suddenly realized the most significant difference between Cheyenne and Peri: one of them was much smarter than the other.

"Anyway, so Tommy is offering him money for me. And not like a lot of money—$500! And instead of telling him to fuck off, Jason was just like, *sure, sounds cool.* What the actual fuck, you know?"

"What a bastard," said Shark, striving to look appropriately shocked. "I would have punched him in the face."

"That," she said, putting her hand on his arm and pressing her breasts into him, "is because you're a real man."

He wondered what her success rate was with that move. Probably pretty good. And five years ago, even when he'd been dating Francesca, he probably would have taken the offer. Instead, he was wondering if there was any beer in his fridge.

"I try," he said, smiling and trying to look impressed. He felt his phone buzz in his pocket, and he pulled it out for a quick check.

BLACK HEARTS ARE A YES.

"Hey, I'm going to grab another drink at the bar. Do you want anything?"

"Another one of these would be great," she said, waggling her Long Island glass and looking smug.

"Back in a flash," he said, already edging away.

Once off the smoking patio, he walked straight out of the bar, handing the mostly full pack of cigarettes to the first bum he saw.

Once home, he shed his accessories, including his gun, and flopped onto the couch with his beer. He left the lights off so he could watch the glow of the city. He found it reassuring—the same way he found the stink of garbage in summer reassuring. It was the way the city changed without ever changing. On his way back from the kitchen for his third beer, his phone buzzed with an incoming text.

He flipped it over and saw a message from Peri.

Which one?

And a picture of two different athletic shoes.

He knew he shouldn't respond. Accidental meetings were one thing, but this was direct contact. Definitely a direct violation of the terms of his agreement with Al. On the other hand, fuck Al.

First ones.

He could see that his text had been received, but there was a long stretch of radio silence.

Sorry. That was supposed to go to Trey.

Shark hated Peri's boyfriend only slightly less now that Trey had moved out-of-state. This didn't help any. He wanted her to be texting him or calling him. Or screw both of those, it was Saturday night—they should be on the couch with Netflix and chill. Other twenty-somethings had that. He had it on good authority that there was actual chilling that happened to actual people. Why couldn't one of those people be him? On a three-beer-driven impulse, he typed in the first thing that came to mind.

In that case, your sexting is terrible.

He waited. Nothing. He knew he should let it go, but instead he typed a second message.

You know you laughed.

This time, the response was immediate: Not that I'm admitting to you.

In the dark, he grinned at his phone. Whatever else might be between them, she still thought he was funny.

There was a ping and a picture of fire. Then one of a pot of boiling water. Finally, words: I'M SENDING YOU HOT AND STEAMY PICTURES. IS THAT BETTER?

He choked a little on his beer as he laughed. Then quickly typed and hit send.

GARBAGE. TRASH. LITTER. SHOWER SCUM.

He waited to see if she got it.

ARE YOU TALKING DIRTY TO ME? AND SHOWER SCUM, REALLY?

TOO MUCH?

YOU'RE SO WEIRD.

YOU STARTED IT.

I'M GOING AWAY NOW.

NIGHT.

He waited. A long minute later, a message came through.

NIGHT.

Sunday ~ March 12

Shark: Pomona Heights

Shark approached Tommy's house and parked next to the most boring sedan in the world. It was so dull it couldn't even pick a color of bland. Was it beige? Was it gray? Who could tell? It would probably be really soothing to look at while on acid.

He'd had to do some deep digging on the douchebags collective pages to find photos tagged to Tommy and Tommy's house. From there, Google Maps Street View had taken him the rest of the way.

Pomona Heights was a once-elitist neighborhood that was slowly sliding toward just another housing development. The houses still had all the matching paint schemes, but the enforcement of yard care was clearly slipping, and the security guard shack at the gate was no longer manned. The houses were all two-story, trying to look three—the architecture trying to make each home look more grandiose than it was.

Tommy's house certainly wasn't helping keep up appearances—it looked even more distressed than it had from Google. He made his way through the overgrown side yard to the pool in the back. The pool looked in need of a cleaning and had underwear floating in it. From his angle, he could see that the sliding doors from the living room were open.

"Fine," he heard a voice say, "I guess we'll just have to do this the hard way."

He paused to assess if he was having another acid flashback.

"No, no, no," whined another voice, a man's voice. Shark shook his head and rounded the edge of the house, walking into the living room.

Peri had her knife in one hand and a junkie duct taped to a rather nice mid-century Danish modern dining chair. He looked more skinny and strung out than his social media pictures, but it was definitely Tommy with his ratty long hair tied in a man bun.

"Huh," said Shark, surveying the scene. "Surprising, yet also familiar."

Peri was eyeing him suspiciously.

"Oh, thank God. Man, you gotta call the cops. You gotta help me. The bitch is crazy. She's going to cut me." Tommy was babbling. Shark circled the room, noting the fully cooked needle of heroin ready to go on the table next to the couch.

"You can't cut him," said Shark.

"Yes, tell her," said the man.

Shark circled around behind Peri. Now that he didn't have Peri's ass distracting him, he was pretty sure he had a lock on the rules of the game, and really, there was only one rule.

Rule one: touching, but no participating.

Nope.

Rule two: no talking about anything serious.

Not really.

Rule one: only players get to play.

He dropped a kiss on the exposed area of skin between her shoulder and her neck. She leaned back against him, and he rested his hand on her hip.

"Cutting won't work. He's a junkie. Blood doesn't scare them. And if he bleeds too much, he'll pass out."

"Well, what do you suggest?" she demanded. "I asked Tommy nicely, and he won't cooperate."

"Is that true, Tommy?" asked Shark. "What's the matter? Don't you want to be cooperative?"

Tommy was sweating. "I'm trying to cooperate. I just don't know what you're talking about, man. I'm just the house sitter! Drugs and whatever? I mean, sure, I use, but I don't know anything."

"You see, what you need," said Shark, "is something painful that won't leave a lot of evidence." He left Peri and walked over to Tommy. "Something that makes an impression."

He reached out, grasped one of Tommy's fingers, and twisted it until he felt the crack.

Tommy screamed.

"Shhhh," said Peri, holding one finger up to her lips. "You'll worry the neighbors." She was wearing a pair of incredibly sexy little fashion gloves. He wondered if he could talk her into wearing those and nothing else.

"The nice thing is," said Shark, focusing back on Tommy, "you've got nine more to work with."

"Not to mention toes," said Peri, smiling at Tommy. "Don't forget the toes."

"What one should I do next?" asked Shark, as Peri came to stand next to him. They both scrutinized Tommy's body.

"Do one from the other hand," said Peri. "That way, if he lives through this, he won't be able to shoot up."

"Jesus," gasped Tommy, "you're so fucking mean."

"And so fucking hot," said Shark, staring at Peri in amazement. That hadn't even occurred to him.

Tommy was panting in panic and pain. Peri stretched out a hand and poked at the broken finger with interest. Tommy leaned away from her, turning his face away, his eyes squinting in terror.

"I don't think he agrees with you," said Peri.

Shark grabbed Tommy by the bun and twisted his head to look directly at Peri. "You don't think my girl is hot?" he demanded.

"Man, can we just..."

Shark grabbed Tommy's ear and torqued it, which made Tommy scream and Peri laugh.

"I asked a question," hissed Shark. "Do you think she's hot?"

"No," screamed Tommy. "No, I think she's a fucking psychotic angel of death!"

"Good job, Tommy," said Shark, leaning down to stare into Tommy's face. Peri draped herself over Shark's shoulder—she was watching Tommy with an intense fascination. "See? You *can* answer questions. Now let's keep the ball rolling."

"I don't know nothing, man," wailed Tommy.

"You take delivery of the drugs from Javelina," said Peri. Shark's ears perked up. As usual, Peri knew things he didn't. "Then what happens?"

"What do you think happens?" muttered Tommy.

"I think," said Shark, "that up until recently you would divide it up and sell it to the three douchebags Jason, Erik, and Vic. Tell us where you send the money. You're not keeping the cash. Where does it go?"

Tommy shook his head. Shark reached for the first finger on Tommy's other hand.

"You don't understand. They will fucking kill me!"

"You know," said Peri conversationally, "I've heard that losing a pinky toe can severely affect balance. Like to the point you have to relearn how to walk. I've never had a chance to test it out."

"Oh Jesus," wailed Tommy.

"Answer the question, Tommy," said Shark, "Or I'll let my angel decide what to do next."

"There's a guy who does a pick up once a week. He comes up in a U-Haul. I don't know his name. He just comes. I don't have any drugs or money, man. I'm supposed to get a new delivery this week, but Javelina hasn't called. I don't know what happened. But if you want shit, go see her."

"You don't know what happened? I'll tell you what happened. They're cutting you out," said Shark.

"Guess they're still mad you lost an entire key," said Peri. Again, Peri had information he didn't. Why didn't he just start every project by talking to her first?

"I got that back," protested Tommy.

"Yes, but you left a mess, didn't you, Tommy?" asked Peri

through gritted teeth. Against his shoulder, Shark could feel that her body was rigid.

"I don't know what you're talking about," said Tommy, avoiding eye contact.

She kicked him—hard—in the chest, and the chair went flying over. Tommy landed with a solid smack that left him coughing. A problem not helped when Peri jumped onto his chest.

"You left her in a ditch," she said, her face inches away from Tommy's. Shark squatted down next to them. He'd never seen her this visibly angry. The blade of her knife caressed Tommy's face.

"It was her fault," panted Tommy, trying to get air back into his lungs. "We were partying, and I thought she'd like this one guy. He paid me like $400 to set them up. I thought she'd be into it and we could split the cash."

"You pimped her out," said Peri.

"I thought she'd be into it. The other girls were into it. But she freaked, and she left, and she took the drugs with her. And I had to have the shit. Jason was on his way up. I couldn't not have it. You don't know these people. You have to make the payments on time."

"What did you do, Tommy?"

"It was Preston," whined Tommy desperately. "All she had to do was give him the damn shit. It was right there in her car, but she wouldn't stop freaking out. It was her fault."

"You shot her," said Peri, and Tommy tried to shake his head, but stopped when he ran into her knife.

"No, no, no. That was Preston. She wouldn't let go of the bag."

"So you let him shoot her."

"I didn't know he was going to do it, man. He just did it! But she was alive when I left. Someone could have stopped and helped her."

Shark looked at Peri's face. He wasn't sure how much time he had left to get the information out of Tommy.

"Give me a name," said Shark. "Who do you make the payments to?"

"The guy in the U-Haul," gasped Tommy. "It's just the guy in the U-Haul."

"Not good enough," said Peri. She put her knife directly above his eye. Every time Tommy blinked, his eyelashes brushed up against it. He gaped like a fish trying to take in air.

"Who tells the U-Haul to come?" demanded Shark.

"Preston," he said at last. "He's the one who set up this gig. He's in real estate. Preston Peccary. That's all I know."

"The guy from the bus stops?" asked Peri, her knife not wavering.

"Yes, that's the guy, and I swear that's all I know," said Tommy. "That's it." His eyes slid toward Shark, but he didn't dare turn his head. "Please. I told you everything."

Shark rubbed his chin. The muscles in Peri's forearm were bunched like cables. He couldn't tell if it was taking everything she had to stab him or everything she had to stop herself. It was possible that she didn't know.

"Think carefully about this, little bird," he said quietly. "You can't undo this."

"He left her in a ditch to bleed to death," said Peri.

"I'm not saying he doesn't deserve it. And whatever you want to do," said Shark, "I will back you. But think carefully."

Tears were leaking out of Tommy's eyes, but he didn't have the air to actually cry.

"There's a reason you don't do shoot for hire," he said.

"But I could," she said.

"Of course you could. That's why you don't do it. You don't want to be that person. It's a thin line, but it is a line. Do what you need to do, just be sure you're not making a choice you'd regret."

The room was silent. Outside, he heard a lone bird call.

Peri stood up and walked out of the room. Moments later, he heard the front door slam.

"Whew," said Shark, setting Tommy upright. "The angel of death almost had you on that one. You got lucky there, Tommy."

Tommy sobbed to himself.

"But here's the problem," said Shark. "I love my little angel, and I can't have anyone else knowing she was here." He walked over to the couch and picked up the syringe full of heroin. "So what if we just give you a little medicine to make you forget? You'd like that, right?"

"Yes," sobbed Tommy, watching the syringe.

Shark undid the good hand and handed him the syringe. Tommy immediately injected it into the arm that was still strapped to the chair. Shark picked up his chin and looked into eyes that were quickly dulling.

"If you tell anyone about her," said Shark, "I will kill you. Do you understand?"

"Yes," said Tommy.

"Good," said Shark.

He took out his phone, activated the record app, and dialed Vivian. "I've got a junkie for you in Pomona Heights. He can testify about the Scarecrow's pipeline. Well," he glanced back at Tommy's half-closed eyes, "maybe. If you can sober him up."

"I don't care about them," said Vivian. "I care about Geier."

"Your friend Ryan cared, and I thought the more bad guys you take down, the better you'd look. But hell, if you guys don't care, then I can let him go."

There was a silence on the other end of the line. He waited.

"Give me the address," she said, coming back.

"I'll text you," said Shark. "Don't come in lights blazing or anything. It would be nice if you could try not to totally blow my cover for once."

"Fuck you," said Vivian.

"You already did," said Shark. "I was under the impression you enjoyed it. I'm leaving him duct taped to a chair, so no need to rush."

He hung up the phone and turned back to Tommy.

"The cops are coming," he lied. The junkie twitched. "They'll be here in an hour or less. That means methadone for you. But that means it's easier for me to find you and kill you. Blink if you understand me."

Tommy blinked.

Shark texted the address and went out front. It might work out for Tommy.

Peri was standing on the front lawn, staring down the hill

toward the entrance of the neighborhood. Her arms were folded around herself, and he couldn't tell from her back if she was mad at him or not.

He approached carefully. This was the difficult part. When they stopped playing and had to start being themselves.

She spun around and pushed herself against him, burying her face against his chest. He wrapped his arms around her and exhaled. Neither of them moved. The longer they stood there, the more he could feel the knots in his back start to untangle.

Eventually, she turned her head to one side so she could talk. "Thanks," she said. He kissed the side of her head, which was currently all that was available to him. "But," she said, looking up at him, "something will have to be done with him."

"Don't worry about it," he said. "I called some people." She nodded. "However, it sounds like we should have a conversation about what each of us knows about Tommy and his friends."

"I'll show you mine if you show me yours?"

"I was thinking more like lunch, but whatever works for you."

She smiled, still not in a laughing mood. "There's a diner—Little Jerry's—it's a couple of exits away. Marko says it's acceptable."

"Then we know it will be delicious. Drive you?"

"No, uh," she blushed, "I bought a car."

She turned and pointed to the gray sedan.

"Oh," said Shark, staring at the vehicle. "You... bought... a car."

She burst out laughing. "You were so manfully restrained just then. It's OK. You can say it: my car is vehicular birth control."

"It does look very, uh, safe."

"Don't worry," she said. "I won't ever make you ride in it. Meet you at the diner?"

16

Shark: Little Jerry's

The diner was exactly what Shark had expected from a Marko recommendation. The outside was struggling to hold up paint, but it was surrounded by cars even at this odd hour of the day, and he could see through the window that the booths were full. There was also a state patrol car in the parking lot as he pulled in, but Peri's hideous vehicle was already parked. He entered the diner and scanned the interior. A pair of state troopers were seated toward the front, where they could keep an eye on their car, and were midway through their burgers.

Peri waved to him from a booth at the back. He hung up his coat on the hook at the end of the bench seat and slid in beside her so that he could keep his back to the wall and, if he were really honest, be next to her. There was a cup of coffee already waiting for him. She had a tall glass of water.

"The special is a corned beef sandwich," she said, looking up from the menu. "Because of course it is. I'm not sure why everyone suddenly gets all *they're after me Lucky Charms* this time of year."

He laughed and wanted to kiss her just for being down on St. Patrick's day, but refrained.

"And I said you'd want decaf. She said you could swap it if you wanted."

He glanced at his watch and shrugged.

"My schedule's so fucked up these days, it doesn't really matter." He took in the water again. "No Coke for you?"

"I've had a hard time sleeping lately," she said, bending over the menu. "I'm trying to cut back." He frowned, uncertain whether or not to inquire further. "Marko said the burgers were good here. But I was thinking about maybe an omelet."

"What does he do when I'm not around? Just drive around and try out new restaurants?"

"Yes, I think so." She flashed a look up at him, full of laughter. He stretched out his legs under the table and put his arm along the back of the booth. She turned toward him, pulling her feet up onto the bench and leaning back, so that her cheek was resting against his arm. "Honestly, anymore, if I need a recommendation, I just text him. He should start a blog," she said, and Shark laughed. "What? He should."

"The Wise Guy Reviews? I'm sure every cop in the area would follow it."

Peri shrugged. The waitress circled back around to take their order. He watched Peri deliberate over omelet toppings. Was ham better than bacon? Which cheese? He wondered if he should have just killed Tommy. Would threats and heroin hold? It was a risk and, more than a risk to him, it was a risk to Peri. On the other hand, he needed to make some things happen. Giving Tommy to Vivian should do the trick, one way or another.

The waitress went away, and Peri looked at him with one eyebrow popped up.

"You're worrying over there," she said.

"Just pondering our problems," he hedged. She propped her elbow on the table and set her chin on her hand, staring at him. It was unnerving.

"Something funny?" she asked when he started to smile.

"Just realizing why people don't like it when I stare at them."

"Guilty conscience?"

Direct hit. Damn, she was too good at this. He tweaked her braid, wishing she would lean back again. Limited contact, even through a shirt sleeve, was better than no contact.

"You are allowed to touch me," she said, looking down at his hand. He pulled it back, putting it back along the edge of the booth.

"Not in public with two state troopers in the place," he said, wishing she'd stop reading his mind.

"I have an ID in my wallet that says I'm twenty-one," she said. "It also says my name is Dinah Sparrows, but we can ignore that."

"Dinah?" he repeated. He liked Peregrine. It was interesting and different. Dinah was a terrible name. She laughed.

"Like I said, we can ignore that. Or we can switch to Patience Wren."

"No," he said flatly.

"I've got more. I could keep going."

"Please don't."

She laughed and finally leaned back into his arm.

Her phone buzzed on the table. Without trying, he could see it was a text from Trey. She picked it up, not even trying to hide it.

Are we still on for tonight?

She responded immediately. You bet. Call you tonight at 8. MY TIME. Just to be clear. ;)

She put the phone down and stared at it thoughtfully, while he considered who he knew in California that could accidentally run over Trey.

"This would be easier if I had my own place, wouldn't it?"

Shark found his thoughts slammed into a brick wall. He hadn't even considered that possibility. And what did she mean by bringing it up now, after texting Trey?

"What?" he asked, clearing his throat slightly.

"My birthday is next month, and then graduation is in June. After that, it's college."

He mulled over the possibilities of an unencumbered Peri. Was that better for him? Certainly, it would be easier to avoid Al. What about Vivian? Did it do him any good with Vivian? Maybe.

Maybe was the kind of thing that got men through prison.

"It's not like I can exactly go into a dorm," continued Peri.

Shark tried to picture that. His understanding of dorms was limited, but he assumed they were like a mash-up of prison and every college movie ever, and if that were even partially true, then it would not work out for Peri at all.

"That would probably be bad," he said.

"Right? Where would I keep my knives? And I don't think they have check boxes on the roommate matching forms for *doesn't mind if you come home covered in blood.*" Shark started to laugh, and she grinned as she fiddled with the end of her braid.

"I'm just saying, if I maintain my current lifestyle, then I need to get my own place."

"Where are you going to go?" he asked, realizing that *college* didn't necessarily mean college here. He took a sip of her water to cover his unease.

"Trey wants me to go to California," she said, frowning at her braid. Shark tried to breathe normally. "But I don't think that's a good idea." Shark gently and carefully set the water down. He wanted to suggest the university in the city, but what did he know about colleges?

"The University here would be the easiest. But I can't seem to make a decision. You'd think I would have all this settled because I'm a bit of a planner."

"I had noticed."

"But I just kept putting it off, and now it's here. And I hate that I have to decide so soon."

"June is not exactly tomorrow," he said, while thinking that June was much closer than he could have hoped.

"Acceptance letters go out at the end of the month. So I need to decide soon. But whatever I decide, I'll probably move right after graduation because I'll want to take a few summer classes wherever I go. I'm sure I'll be missing a few requirements because of the transfer."

"What transfer?"

"Well, between my Advanced Placement classes and the Running Start program, I'll be graduating with a high-school diploma and most of an AA."

He stared at her in disbelief. "Running Start?" he repeated.

"It's the program where high school kids can take classes from the local community college for free. So essentially, wherever I go, I'll be transferring in as a junior."

"My high school didn't have art. Our sports gear was from 1989. The last bell rang, and the teachers scattered like cockroaches. And they just let you take college classes?"

"Yes." She had the decency to look somewhat embarrassed.

"I had to study for my English 201 final during a fucking prison riot," he blurted out. "Do you know how hard it is to read Romeo and Juliet while a bunch of inmates chant *Kill the pigs*?"

"Not really, but it sounds hard. How'd you do?"

"I got a fucking *A*! Like I'm going to go through that and not fucking nail it?"

"I find that…" she hesitated as if looking for the right word, "impressive," she said at last.

Somehow that made it better. Not a lot. But a little bit. He shook his head. "I'm just having a moment of cosmic unfairness here."

"I'm sorry," she said.

"Not your fault. But shit," he shook his head again, "life really isn't a level playing field."

"No," she said. "But that just makes you amazing."

He hadn't blushed since he was twelve, but he found that he was fighting the urge to now. The waitress arrived with their food, much to his relief.

"Holy cow!" said Peri, staring at her enormous omelet. "How am I supposed to eat all that?"

"One bite at a time?" he suggested, which made the waitress laugh.

"You're lucky you're cute," she said, pointing her fork at him threateningly.

"You two holler if you need anything," said the waitress, still laughing as she left.

He waited until the waitress was out of earshot before speaking again. "Tell me about Emblem and Tommy and Javelina."

"I'll try. What do you want to know?"

"I've been trying to go back up the pipeline. Jason, Erik, and Vic, the guys from Emblem that your mini-skirts did the bag drop for, are smaller dealers who're trying to make it to mid-level. The deal at Emblem was them trying to move up, right?"

She nodded. "I think so. But I haven't been looking at them."

"The Preston guy Tommy mentioned, what's the deal with him and bus stops? This is the second story I've heard about him trying to buy a girl, and the second time I've heard him referred to as *the bus stop guy*."

She gave him an exasperated look. "You don't ride the bus much, do you?"

"Not if I can help it," said Shark.

"Must be nice. Anyway, he's got his ad on every bus stop from here to the city. *Preston Peccary – Pick a friend in realty*. We'll talk about the buying girls in a minute. Let's finish up on the drugs first. What's your interest?"

"Rivals," said Shark. "They're the same people that Fowler was selling to—Scarecrow Jack."

"That tracks," she said, nodding.

"I want to find their network, shut them down."

She looked as if she were about to say something, then changed her mind. "Do you remember the Happy Place Youth Center?"

"Yeah, you said Agent Fowler was pushing it when he did his career day talk." The now deceased ATF Agent Fowler had been selling drugs and weapons out of a federal evidence lock-up. Shark had taken him out with Peri's help, but Peri had been convinced that he was some level of molester.

"Yeah, well, Happy Place is being run by a woman named Roseangel Javelina. She's using kids from the center to do bag drops. That's what you saw the other night at Emblem. They're your average middle-class kids, and they rotate them to different locations and different times."

"Difficult to spot," said Shark, seeing the attraction.

"And cheap. Angel is blackmailing the kids, and most of them don't even know what they're really into."

"But if they're not getting paid, then they can't do any actual buys. You couldn't trust them to handle cash," said Shark.

"Exactly. The kids literally just drop off the drugs. They text on delivery and wait for permission to leave."

Shark considered the scheme. "So the buys are on account. The Tommy-type dealers place an order. Then, once the kids confirm delivery, the buyers have to pay up, or else? That means they've got their hooks in the dealers pretty bad. Otherwise, the chance of one of them taking off without paying is pretty high."

She shrugged. "Not my area of expertise. But I haven't been able to tell who's getting the money. Happy Place doesn't receive the cash. I also think she's targeting kids for sex trafficking, but I haven't been able to catch any part of that. Which is why I'm interested to hear that this is the second time you've heard about Preston Peccary trying to buy a girl."

"Sounds like we should target Preston," mused Shark. "If he's the money guy, then he has to know something." Something else was bothering him about the money, but he couldn't quite put his finger on it.

Shark rubbed his chin thoughtfully. As he considered his options, he saw the state troopers stand up and toss their tip on the table. But instead of turning toward the door, they began to walk back toward his table.

Peregrine: Having Kittens

"Hi," said the first state trooper, smiling tightly, ignoring Shark and looking directly at Peri. She maintained eye contact, but she felt Shark drop his hand from the back of the booth to her leg. "You're driving the gray Volvo?"

"Yes?" Peri smiled, trying to look innocent.

"I wanted to let you know that your tabs have expired."

"I forgot to check the tabs," she gasped, turning to Shark, her face flushing red. She felt horribly embarrassed. How could she have forgotten such a simple detail? She stared at Shark, not knowing what to do next. What was the right angle to play?

"She just bought the car a few days ago," said Shark, looking up at the trooper.

Peri felt herself relax. Yes, Shark was right, she just needed to play the scene as is.

"I did," she said, turning to the trooper. She widened her eyes and took a deep breath, like she'd seen Regan do. It was designed to make her cleavage bounce ever so slightly. Her cleavage wasn't as good as Regan's, but she figured it would do. "I didn't even think to check the tabs."

"Did you file the change of ownership?" asked the trooper, his expression set to condescending.

"Yes, I did." She looked around as if she'd misplaced

something and flapped her hands. "My uncle said I should carry copies with me, though. Just in case." She really did have the paperwork in her bag, but she didn't want to actually go through the bag, so she just made pawing motions, like she was going to.

"That's good advice," said the trooper, waving away the bag. "But you should have renewed the tabs at the same time."

"It's the first car I bought on my own! I didn't even think about it! What do I do?"

She tried to look appealingly distressed. She turned toward Shark to get a gauge on her performance. Was it too much? Shark was in full poker face mode—difficult to get a read on.

"It's OK," Shark said. "We'll go to the DMV tomorrow and get you new tabs. It's easy."

She turned to the trooper, as if for approval.

"He's right," said the trooper, smiling in a fatherly fashion. "It's quite easy. There's even a branch a few miles down the road. And since you're only one day over, I'll let you off with a warning."

"Oh, thank you!" She beamed, and the trooper smiled back.

"Well, you two have a nice day," he said, and they turned back to the door.

"Thanks again," she called after them. "And stay safe!"

He waved his acknowledgment, and Peri relaxed back into her seat.

"What a dick," she said as the trooper pulled away. "One day over? Why don't you just go ticket someone in the carpool lane?" She collapsed back against Shark's arm and closed her eyes, suddenly tired.

"Please don't ever pull that one on me," said Shark.

"Which one?" asked Peri, opening one eye to look up at him in surprise.

"The 1000-watt distressed kitten look. You'd have my keys, my wallet, and my bank account numbers in about two seconds flat."

She laughed and closed her eyes again, snuggling against him. "I doubt that."

"What's with the not sleeping?" he asked.

She refused to open her eyes or look up at him, but she knew that he'd noticed her avoidance. "It's fine. I just need to manage my caffeine problem a little better."

"Peregrine," he said, and paused, seeming to pick his words carefully, even as his arm curled around her shoulders, "that's bullshit." She was startled into looking directly at him again. He smiled a sort of embarrassed smile, but his eyes looked worried. How did he manage to look so damn sweet?

Peri sighed. She knew she should sit up and discuss matters like an adult, but leaning against him was the best she'd felt in weeks. He was warm and comfortable, and with his arm around her, she finally felt like she could relax.

"It's this case. It's got under my skin a little. Usually, I can shut stuff down, but this one is tripping me up, I guess. And it doesn't help that my house feels about as secure as a cardboard box." She shook her head. She hadn't meant to say the last part, and she actually made an effort to sit up. He tightened his arm around her shoulders, and she gave in, melting back against him.

"Can you go spend a couple of nights with Al?"

"He doesn't like me to spend the night. He thinks I'm

secretly plotting to move in or something. Which, if you'd ever seen his place, you'd know was ridiculous. I'm just trying to get some damn sleep. Anyway, it's fine. I'm fine. What do you want to do?"

"Nothing appropriate for a diner."

She laughed again. "I meant about Preston Peccary et al. How do you want to divide this up?"

"Mmm, I don't suppose you want to just let me handle it? It would be a lot safer for you if I just took a run at Preston myself."

"Oh my God. You and my uncle should form a fucking club."

"You mean, *The Peregrine Hays Takes Too Many Risks Club*? I'm the Treasurer. Al is President."

She struggled to keep a straight face. "I don't take risks I can't handle. And it might be safer for me, but it would not be safer for you."

"Considering that you have saved my ass on more than one occasion, that is probably true. Let me talk to Marko. Keep your hooks in at Happy Place and see if you can dig up more on Javelina. Right now, I just want to know where the money is going. Once we know that, maybe we can figure out a plan."

She nodded. "Fair enough."

"Are you going to call your uncle about getting you some tabs?"

"Hey, all evidence to the contrary, I can take care of it myself. Plus, he's got some cheating spouse thing, so he had to go to church."

"Run that one by me again?" Shark's scarred eyebrow went up, like it always did when he was skeptical.

"I know. *Al* and *church* didn't really go in the same sentence. He's got a client whose wife has taken a sudden interest in religion. Which could be true, or she could be boffing the deacon while they're *cleaning the church*. He won't be home for another hour or two. But now that I'm thinking of it, can't I renew online?" He nodded. "Also, I need to put in some face time with my mom or she'll start having kittens about how we're not close or something."

He paid the bill, as usual, and walked her out to the car. Peri debated saying something. She deserved an explanation of some kind. She looked up into his face and decided that maybe she was too chicken.

"Angel said to check in with her on Monday, and she'd have an errand for me. Do you want me to call you after?"

"Yes," he said with a nod. "Find out about as many of the deliveries as you can and let me know. I'll talk to Marko tomorrow and hopefully come up with a game plan."

"OK," said Peri, turning to get into the car.

"Hey," he said, reaching out, his hands just grazing the inside of her arm and turning her back to him. "At some point, we'll need to talk about us."

Apparently, he was less chicken than she was.

"I think I'm pretty clear on us," said Peri. "You want me. You want to be with me, but for various reasons that you're refusing to discuss, you won't. In this conversation you want to have, will you be discussing any of those reasons?"

He looked annoyed. "No. Probably not."

"Then why have the conversation?"

He closed his eyes and looked like he was counting to ten. "Because I don't want you to be mad at me. I don't think I can take it. I think my kidney is still bruised from Friday night, if nothing else."

Peri took a breath and tried to formulate what she wanted. Shark. She wanted Shark. But everything else was a jumble. "You know what, you're right. We'll have to talk at some point, but this isn't that point. At least not for me. I can't focus on us right now. Let's just get through this—shut down Angel and Preston—and then we'll…" she waved her hands to try to describe the nebulous concept that was about to be encompassed in a single word, "talk."

He nodded, but didn't look pleased with that response. She waited while he chewed on what he wanted to say. Finally, he simply spit it out. "Peri, all I really need to know is if there is an *us* to talk about."

She hated multiple choice. He couldn't go for essay? Because if the answer was *yes* or *no,* then she had to go with *yes*, but she had a lot of fucking caveats. Vivian alone was worth an entire blue book. And Trey? God damn it, what about Trey? This was exactly the kind of thing she was trying to avoid thinking about. He was watching her. Tick-tock, Peregrine. Make a decision. She felt herself sweating.

"Yes," she said, and to her relief, he stepped in and kissed her, which was a much easier thing to think about.

"Then we can figure everything else out later," he said, letting her go. She swayed slightly on her feet and tried not to look as sprung as she felt. She suspected, from the way he grinned as he opened her car door, that she was not very successful.

Monday ~ March 13

Shark: The Gas Station

Shark attempted to make eggs and dial Marko simultaneously. Eventually, Marko picked up. Shark switched the phone to speaker and put the phone down.

"Hello?" Marko sounded sleepy. And pissed.

"What do you do that makes my eggs not taste like crap?"

"I learned how to cook," said Marko.

"But it's eggs. That shouldn't require a culinary degree. I saw the guys working the kitchen in prison. This cannot be that hard."

"And yet, your eggs look like a runny mess, don't they?"

"I admit nothing, but, theoretically, if they were runny, what would I do about that?"

"Cook them longer. Add more cheese. The cheese will help mitigate the taste of failure."

Shark shrugged and followed directions.

"Was there a reason you were waking me at this un-Godly hour besides consulting on your breakfast?"

"Yes. The Scarecrow Jack gang. I don't know if you've heard, but three of our places got hit here in the city."

"I had heard. I imagine Geier wants to hit back hard?"

"Yes, but that's complicated by the fact that no one knows who Scarecrow Jack is, and we know fuck all about his organization. It's like they just sprang up overnight, but they know the city as well as we do. I'm attempting to gather some information, but I've turned up something that I need your help with." He slid the eggs onto a plate and added a dollop of ketchup in case the cheese didn't help enough.

"Whatever you need. Shoot."

"Remember when we took out Fowler and you guys grabbed the merchandise?"

"Yeah."

"You and Peri and Eddie took out the buyers, and you said that they were driving a U-Haul, right?"

"Yeah, we torched it and ditched it down by the Port."

"And you never turned up anything on the drivers?"

"No, not really. Why?"

"Well, I was chasing down a lead yesterday, and this distributor said that a guy in a U-Haul collects his payments. That seems a bit too coincidental for my tastes. Maybe it wasn't the drivers we should have been looking into, but the vehicle. Did you keep any of their stuff or remember what the license plate was? Maybe we can dig around and find something."

"Hm," said Marko, in a way that Shark didn't like.

"Are you going to expound on that?"

"Yes, but you're not going to like it," said Marko.

"Well, whatever it is, it will probably be better than my eggs."

Marko cleared his throat. "Well, after we took out the guys,

Peri made a point of searching them. Took snaps of their wallet contents and maybe the license plate of the U-Haul. Your instructions were to get rid of everything, and we weren't interested in who they were at the time. So I didn't keep any of it. If you want that information, you're going to have to call her."

"So much for keeping her out of this."

Marko cleared his throat again. "Well, not to stick my oar in the water here, but chances are if she did all that at the time, she was in it ahead of us."

Shark mulled over Marko's point. As usual, he was probably right. But he was also right that Shark didn't like it. Peri had always had her own secrets. How long had she been chasing this? What was Peri not telling him? She was fully capable of running her own shit, but that didn't stop him from worrying. Work and personal were a blurred line that they were speeding by.

"OK, I'll talk to her. Then I'll meet you at the condo. Let's go over the facts and see what we can't put together."

After hanging up with Marko, Shark pulled up info on Preston Peccary. Like a lot of real estate agents, Preston Peccary had the glossy look of someone who believed that appearances sold. Veneers, tan, Brooks Brothers tie. Preston Peccary was beaming in every picture. Shark was considering making an appointment when a text came through.

URGENT MEETING. SAME PLACE AS LAST TIME. 12 PM.

Shark frowned. This was a bit soon for a meeting, even for Vivian. On the other hand, maybe she'd found out something important. He checked his watch and did the math on the drive time to the condo. Maybe he could meet with Vivian, make it to the condo, and get Peri to come by after school. He wasn't sure if there was an official status change between the two of them, but he felt like he'd left things in a good place. At minimum, he thought she'd ditch Trey for him.

Shark made the trip to the gas station and parked like before. The clerk nodded, again like before. But something made Shark hesitate. He entered the back room cautiously.

The cement-floored room with the racks of cleaning supplies and lone rickety table appeared empty as he entered.

"Thanks for coming," said Ryan, stepping forward and locking the door behind Shark. "Wasn't sure you would."

"Where's Vivian?" asked Shark.

"Not here," said Ryan and punched him.

Shark staggered back, bumping into the table.

"All right, now that I've got that out of my system, let's talk about Tommy."

Shark ran his tongue along the inside of his teeth. They all felt sound. "What about him?"

Ryan's eyes widened slightly. "You're not even going to deny it?"

"Come down off the high horse. You needed information. I got you information."

"You got me a dead fucking body! That's not what I needed."

Shark sat down on the edge of the table and folded his arms across his chest. "What are you talking about?"

Ryan pulled a manila folder off the rack of cleaning supplies and opened it. "I'm talking about a dead fucking junkie." He tossed a picture on the table next to Shark—it showed Tommy, rather more blue, wet, and dead than he had been when Shark had left.

"I got black hearts all over the fucking house, a dead junkie duct taped to a chair in the pool, and your thumb print on a syringe in the living room. Vivian's not here to cover for you. You fucking killed him."

Shark stared at the picture and back up at Ryan. "I didn't, actually."

"Fuck you. You tortured him and killed him."

"I broke one finger," said Shark. "Not exactly the most extensive torture ever. And I let him shoot up afterwards. He was alive when I left him."

"Then how did he end up in the pool?"

So that's how it had gone down. Shark had put the balls on the table, left Vivian to play, and that's how it had broken for Tommy. Not that he felt bad about it—it would make Peri happy at least. The only real question was whether or not he could trust Ryan. Time to take a risk. "You should probably ask Vivian that," he said.

"What's that supposed to mean?"

"Geier has me looking into the Scarecrow Jack network. I found Tommy. I asked him some questions about where he got his drugs and where his money went. Then I called Vivian— that's protocol. I told her to call you. I told her that Tommy could testify about the Scarecrows pipeline. Then I left him, duct taped, yes, but very much alive."

Ryan took a step back. "That doesn't make any sense. Why would she kill him?"

Shark waited, letting Ryan fill in his own blanks. Ryan walked to the door and back. "She's been pushing you hard to get in with Geier."

"Yes, but has she filed any reports on the information I've given her? Because two weeks ago, I gave her the addresses of some stash houses. Then, last week, they were both hit by the Scarecrows."

"I don't know about the reports," said Ryan thoughtfully. "I wouldn't have access to those because it's not my case. They've got a pretty high fence around you two. I only got in because of the overlap in the cases. For all I know, you're bullshitting me to get out of murder."

"I called Vivian. You can check it."

"We could pull your phone records," said Ryan, as if testing the idea. "But that won't prove what you talked about."

Shark pulled out his phone. He flipped through his apps and pushed play.

I've got a junkie for you in Pomona Heights. He can testify about the Scarecrow's pipeline. Well, maybe. If you can sober him up.

I don't care about them. I care about Geier.

Your friend Ryan cared, and I thought the more bad guys you take down, the better you'd look. But hell, if you guys don't care, then I can let him go.

Give me the address.

I'll text you. Don't come in lights blazing or anything. It would be nice if you could try not to totally blow my cover for once.

Fuck you.

You already did. I was under the impression you enjoyed it. I'm leaving him duct-taped to a chair, so no need to rush.

"You can check my phone if you want to see the text I sent her," said Shark.

Ryan was looking thoughtful again. "She shot Fowler, didn't she?"

"Yes," said Shark.

"I knew it! Everything was too tidy. At first, I thought she was covering for you, but the more time I spend with her, the more I've been thinking she's the fucking dickhead in your little partnership."

"Thanks," said Shark. "I feel so insulted and validated at the same time."

"Whatever. You know what I mean. You make sense. I'm not saying that breaking people's fingers is OK—it's not. Stop fucking doing that. But it makes sense. She's the one who's acting squirrelly. She's been pushing too hard, and she wants me out too much, and she doesn't like oversight."

"She does not like anyone over her, that is true," agreed Shark. Ryan was staring off into the stacks of potato chips as if considering the situation, and didn't respond. "What are our options?" asked Shark, purposefully using *our*—he needed Ryan to fully commit to being on his side. Ryan smacked the file folder against the palm of his other hand with a repetitive thwap, thwap sound. Shark waited.

"OK, here's the problem," said Ryan. "You're the first guy inside Geier's operation that we've had in six fucking years. His operation is mature, it's producing, and it's high-profile. The

Scarecrows are new and troublesome, but they aren't the big fish that Geier is. If I pull you to testify against Vivian, then we lose you as a witness against Geier. Which is a problem for the Bureau. They won't like it. I mean, they won't like having a dirty agent—period—but disrupting multiple cases will really take the cake."

"But you don't mind?" asked Shark, skeptically.

"Are you kidding? I'm lead on the Scarecrows. If I can get Vivian, I can probably have their whole organization wrapped up by summer. But I can't move against her without evidence. I need something to start an IA investigation. Some sort of evidence of improper behavior to give the guys a reason to go digging."

"That's bullshit," said Shark. "I'm telling you she's dirty."

"Yeah, and I'm telling you that I believe you. But, and no offense, the word of a felon doesn't carry a ton of weight when it comes to accusing an FBI agent."

"That's ridiculous. Wouldn't felons be the ones who would know?"

"I…" Ryan appeared to be at a loss for how to respond. "You know what? Why don't we just focus on finding some sort of evidence?"

Shark ran through a mental index of what he had on Vivian. He really didn't want to bring up the mess on Fowler. Technically, he'd been the one to pull the trigger, so it was going to come down to the he said-she said bullshit that Ryan was looking to avoid. Not to mention that it was too much exposure for Marko and the crew. What did that leave?

"What about the fact that she was sleeping with me?"

"Highly improper, and very... I'd definitely need evidence. Beyond that phone call, I mean."

"What about photographs?"

"She let you take pictures?" Ryan looked both uncomfortable and suspicious.

"She doesn't know about the pictures."

"You took pictures without her knowing? Dude, that's so not cool. I don't care what kind of crazy she is."

"I didn't know about them either!"

"Someone else took pictures? What the hell?"

Shark started to try to explain and then realized it was going to be a swamp of alternative facts. "It's a long story, and we don't have the time, so never mind. But if I could get them, would that be enough? And would you have to say where you got them?"

"Probably not initially. I could say they were given to me by a CI."

"OK," said Shark, nodding. "I think I can do that."

"That's great. Meanwhile, your handler is fucking killing people. You do know what happens if she figures out you're on to her, right?"

"Same thing that happens if someone realizes I'm working for the FBI. But welcome to my life."

"Your life sucks," said Ryan, looking worried.

"It has its bright spots," said Shark. "Now what do you know about a guy named Preston Peccary?"

"The guy on all the bus stops?"

"Am I the only one who never looks at bus stop

advertising? Yes, him. Tommy said that he was the money guy for the Scarecrows."

"I'll look into him. But I think we should focus on Vivian."

"No, we can't," said Shark. "She's going to do what she's always done. She's going to push me for more details on Geier's organization. If I can stall long enough, then I can figure out the Scarecrows' network, and between you and me and Geier, we can squish them like bugs before Vivian figures out what the fuck is going on."

Ryan was looking doubtful. "Christ, kid… Maybe I should just pull you in. We can sort out Vivian and take another run at Geier later."

"You just said the Bureau wouldn't like that."

"Who cares what they like as long as you don't get shot?"

"And what happens to my deal if you pull me in?"

Ryan shifted on his feet, and the folder thwapped into his palm again. "The deal will have to be adjusted. It wouldn't be null, but yeah, it would have to be sorted out."

"And while it's being sorted out, I'll be back in prison, right?"

Ryan made a face, like he wished it wasn't true. "Yeah, probably. Probably in isolation to protect you from retaliation."

Shark thought about his options. He wasn't stupid. An investigation against Vivian, his deal, testifying… all of that could take a year. Maybe he'd get lucky and a lawyer could get him out earlier, but the odds weren't good. Meanwhile, Geier would be hunting for him. In prison, Geier had a hundred guys he could reach out to, and Shark would only have to be unlucky once. He thought about Peri. That was the point of this whole arrangement, right? To get out of it with a real life. Somehow, that now included Peri. He couldn't do another year.

"No," said Shark. "I didn't come all this way for nothing. I can do this."

Ryan stared at him. Shark stared back. "Fucking balls of steel on you, kid. OK, we'll do it your way. Get me those pictures ASAP. The sooner I can start the ball rolling on Vivian, the sooner I can get you the fuck out of here."

"I'll work on it. Meanwhile, Preston Peccary. Start digging. I need to know everything about him. Also, I need an alias with a good credit rating."

"What?"

"He's a real estate agent with his face on every fucking bus stop. I figured I'd give him a call and see if I can't get him to show me some condos. But he's not going to show me crap if I'm not ready to ball. I need him to think that I'm his type of person—the type of person who might need to be shown a good time. I can't use my name. If he really was Fowler's buyer, then he's going to know who I am."

"Oh, for Christ's sake. If the Bureau ends up buying you a condo, I'm going to be so fucking annoyed."

Shark grinned. "I don't need the actual condo, I just need to have the credit rating to make me look like a real buyer."

"All right, I'll see what I can do." Ryan dug into his pocket and pulled a square-ish block of a phone—dial only, no smart tech—and handed it to Shark. "My number is pre-programmed on this. You can call me anytime. Anything else?"

Shark blinked. "No?" He wasn't used to having a handler who actually wanted to help him.

Ryan laughed. "Just stay alive, kid. We'll take care of the rest."

Shark: Uncle Al's

Shark cruised by Al's apartment, slowing to school zone speeds to clock what was parked in front. He needed to talk to Peri and Marko, but his conversation with Ryan had given him a new set of goals—and problems.

He'd only been to Al's place once before at Peri's direction and never inside, but after Al's visit, he'd made a point of investigating the private investigator. The irate forty-something lived across from a convenience store, about twenty minutes away from Peri, and appeared to exist on take-out and coffee. Not that Shark could look down on him for that. Not everyone was lucky enough to have a Marko. Al didn't look home. Shark checked his watch and made a decision. He parked down the block and walked up to the duplex.

He was feeling the unaccustomed feeling of hope. If Ryan really could help him get out from under Vivian's thumb, he might actually come out of this in one piece. And if he wasn't in prison and he wasn't dead and he wasn't spending his every waking moment looking over his shoulder, then maybe he could tell Al where to stick his goddamn pictures.

It took him a little longer than he would have liked to pick the lock on Al's apartment. He was rusty. Once inside, he made a quick tour of the rooms and then came back to the living room.

He'd found the gun hidden under the mattress and the one behind the toilet, and the one in the office. There was a dusty bottle of Elijah Cook in the cupboard and three days' worth of takeout leftovers in the fridge. The place was poorly arranged and annoyingly clean, but also cluttered. There was an American flag inside a case above the fireplace with a string of medals and a little name plate that read: CHRIS HAYS. He'd never asked Peri about her father, but at least this explained why she never mentioned him.

It was a two-bedroom apartment. One room acted as an office, and the other was Al's actual bedroom. Shark tried the office first. He opened the filing cabinet and began rifling through it, looking for photos of himself. It took him longer than he would have liked to admit to find that Al had filed them under Shark's real name. Because of course he had. Shark pulled them out and then stopped. The hard copies were all well and good, but if Al ever bothered to check the file, he was going to know damn well who had taken the photos.

His phone rang, causing him to jump. He checked the number and saw that it was either Vivian or Ryan. He wished the FBI wouldn't route all their calls through a central line. It was such an easy tell. On the other hand, anyone who knew that also had the FBI on speed dial, so maybe it wasn't a problem.

"Hello?" he asked, picking up.

"Where the hell are you?" demanded Vivian. "I just drove by your place and you're not there."

"I'm not in the city. I had to talk to Marko. I'm in the 'burbs for the night. Why? Are you worried about me?"

"I'm worried about the fact that we have put six months of work into this case, and you haven't come up with anything concrete."

"I'm working on it," said Shark.

"You keep saying that," she said. "I'm not seeing a lot of results."

"I plan on having something for you by the next time we meet. Names."

"You'd better," she said and hung up.

Shark exhaled in frustration and looked down at the photos in his hand. He was tempted to keep the one of him and Peri. It was just the two of them walking and looking happy. He'd burned the copy that Al had given him, and he knew it was the right decision at the time, but he still wanted it. He put it back reluctantly. The picture of Vivian in her underwear and his shirt, he'd happily burn twice over, but that went back in the file too. What he needed was the original photo files.

Shark closed the file drawer and went to the computer. There was a password, of course. Shark typed in: PEREGRINE. But it didn't budge. PERI yielded the same results. Shark then typed in: CHRIS. The computer sprang to life. He rifled through the desktop looking for a filing system. The filing system was as orderly as Al's apartment, which was to say not at all. Shark finally gave up and ran a search based on image files and dates they would have been uploaded.

When he found them, he logged into his email and sent them to Ryan. Then he deleted the browser history and closed down the computer. Shark looked around the room. All the things that mattered to Al were clean and precisely ordered. All the things that he didn't care about seemed casually left around. The stack of mail that was too easy to bump into. The dish towel almost falling off the cabinet handle. He wondered if Al was really messy or if this was his way of detecting snoopers.

On impulse, Shark grabbed the couch and maneuvered it into a better position. Then pushed the coffee table to match. Then he moved the TV out of the back light and glare from the living room windows and into a position against the wall. The guy really needed a chair to complete the new arrangement, but he had the feeling that the guy really needed a lot of things.

He went to the cupboard, got out the bottle of bourbon and a glass, and went back to the couch to wait.

Thirty minutes later, he heard Al's key in the lock. Shark had left it unlocked, just as Al had done to him. And just as Shark had done, Al came in cautiously with his gun drawn.

Al took in the room, Shark, and, last of all, the glass of bourbon in Shark's hand.

"You son of a bitch! Now she's going to think I started drinking again!"

"Oh," said Shark, taking a drink, "I'm sorry. Am I fucking up your relationship with Peregrine? Damn, that must be so annoying."

Al's eyes narrowed in hatred. "You have ten seconds to explain why I'm not shooting you."

"I needed to talk to you."

"Talk fast," said Al.

Shark brushed off an imaginary speck of dust on his knee.

"I saw Peri yesterday."

He watched with interest as the knuckles on Al's gun hand turned white.

"Was I less than clear last time?" demanded Al through clenched teeth.

"Relax," said Shark. "It was work-related. I needed to talk to her."

"And why would you possibly need to talk to her?"

Shark stared at the older man. Who did he think he was fooling?

"Because she's an incredibly talented asset who knows things. And sometimes I need to know things."

"She is not an asset," yelled Al, slamming his gun down on the table with a loud thump.

"Opinions vary," said Shark, taking another sip. "Anyway, my point is that I don't need you finding out about it and popping up to fuck over my life at the worst moment."

"Fine," said Al. "Message delivered. Go away."

Shark exhaled and rubbed the top of his ear.

"Something else on your mind? Besides my furniture placement?"

"This is for your own good," said Shark, pointing to the room. "Also, buy a damn chair. How can you have anyone over with only a couch?"

"Fuck you," said Al. "Spit it out. Whatever you have to say, just say it, so you can leave."

Shark stared at Al. He wasn't sure about this part.

"When I talked to Peri..."

"What?"

"She's tired," said Shark.

"Excuse me?"

"She's not sleeping. Whatever she's working on, it's bugging her. She's not sleeping. I don't think she feels safe at her mom's house."

"And I don't think my niece's sleeping habits are any of your concern," said Al.

Shark stood up angrily. Grabbing the bottle and glass, he carried them to the dining table and set them down in front of Al.

"People who are tired make mistakes. People who make mistakes, get dead. Part of our little arrangement—the reason I'm letting you get away with this shit—is the understanding that you would be taking care of her."

"And I suppose you think you can do a better job?"

It was Shark's turn to clench his teeth. "Yeah, I do." For a moment, he really thought Al would take a swing.

"Get out," said Al.

"Gladly," said Shark.

He was barely out of the door when he heard the bourbon bottle break against the door. He tried not to feel smug about that.

Peregrine: The Real Story

Peri checked her phone as she got out of Chastity. As usual, Shark's text had left her wondering what was going on. He hadn't sent any additional information.

WORK RELATED. NEED TO TALK. HAVE QUESTIONS.

Their last conversation had left her both more and less confused. More confused about her relationship status and less confused about her feelings. Was he as confused as she was? Maybe that was what his text had meant? That he wanted to talk work stuff, and she wouldn't have to think complicated thoughts? Did that mean there wasn't going to be any making out? Well, she'd talked him out of that one before. She could do it again.

She jogged up the stairs to Shark's condo and knocked a quick rat-a-tat-tat on the door. He opened the door and grinned at her.

"You're quick."

"The Peregrine Hays Corporation delivers in under thirty minutes, or your next pizza is free."

"Really? Can I place a delivery order for next week now?" he asked, pulling her inside and wrapping his arms around her. She laughed as he began to pepper her face with kisses.

"OK, OK," she said, leaning back and eyeing him suspiciously. "You're too happy. You're never this happy. What happened?"

"You're here. I'm here. And for fucking once, no one else is here."

Peri laughed again. "Good point. But aren't we supposed to be talking business?"

"Yeah, yeah," he said, letting her go and going back toward the kitchen. "Fine, business first."

Peri dropped her bag on the couch. She wasn't sure what had gotten into him, but she liked happy Shark. Not that she thought of him as unhappy—just generally tense.

"Do you want something?" he asked, pulling a soda out of the fridge and holding it up.

"No thanks," she said. He opened the soda with a sharp, watery snap. "Actually," she said, changing her mind. "I don't suppose there are snacks? I managed to miss lunch today due to a thing."

Shark made a face and opened a cupboard. "We may actually be ordering pizza. I don't know what I have in here."

She leaned against the counter and checked out his ass as he leaned down to check a bottom cupboard. It was ridiculous, logistically problematical, and socially unacceptable, but she always had the desire to bite it. Not hard, just enough to make him jump. "Chex-mix?" he offered, coming back up with a bag in hand, and she pulled her gaze upward.

"Were you checking me out?" he asked, laughing at her. She made an innocent expression and wordlessly shrugged. "I feel used," he said. He leaned in to kiss her, his arms sliding around her again, pulling her against him. "Cheap." He kissed her again and then moved to her neck which always made her melt.

"Dirty?" she suggested, and ran her tongue around the edge of his ear.

He stepped back and took a moment. "That is not going to get us through the business at hand."

She giggled and reached for the Chex-mix. "Depends on what the business is," she said hopping up on the kitchen counter.

"Sadly, it's actual business."

"Then I call this meeting of the Tooth and Talon to order. The Tooth has the floor."

He laughed at her. "The Tooth? That's what I get? Just one?"

She giggled. "I just get one claw. What's the business at hand? Criminal, I hope."

"Isn't it always with us?"

"Not always," she protested. "Sometimes we go whole minutes without doing something in flagrant disregard of the law."

"It seems like I ought to feel bad about that," he said, taking his soda to the table. He sat down and leaned back in his chair, putting his feet up on the chair opposite.

"Meh. I say don't bother."

He raised his can in a silent toast of agreement. "Anyway," he said taking a sip, "I need to talk about something that Tommy said."

Peri crunched a handful of Chex-mix and tried to look more inquiring and less like a chipmunk.

"Tommy said that the money was collected by a guy in a U-Haul. And last night it occurred to me that this isn't the first time the Scarecrows have used a U-Haul. The buyers for Fowler's merchandise were also driving a U-Haul, weren't they?"

Peri nodded thoughtfully and was annoyed at herself for having missed that detail. She'd gotten too hung up on Tommy.

"They did," she said.

"I talked to Marko and he said that you took pictures of wallets and maybe the license plate."

"Didn't get the license plate," she said. "But it was definitely a rental."

"How do you know? What if it was just some guys who bought used U-Hauls?"

"Asked my uncle about that," she said, reaching for more chex-mix. "First, U-Hauls never get sold with their graphics on. Second, it had barcodes on the windows."

Shark stood up and began to wander around the room.

"What does that mean?"

"Rentals almost always have barcodes on the windows, so they can be scanned in and out of the lot. That U-Haul had them on both passenger and driver side windows."

Shark was doing the frowning thing he did when he was trying to work a problem.

"What about the contents of their wallets?"

Peri pulled out her phone and flipped through her files until she found the photos she'd taken. She handed the phone to him. She'd looked at the photos dozens of times. Nothing had ever come to the front as being important.

He walked away with her phone and stared at the pictures while leaning against the doors out to the balcony. "There's not a lot here," he said shaking his head.

"I know," she agreed.

"But you're my goddamn magical unicorn. You're supposed to have all the answers."

Peri burst out laughing. "You give me the weirdest compliments."

He looked out the window toward the parking lot, partially laughing, partially embarrassed.

"Shit," Shark stepped away from the windows. He looked around the room and scooped up her bag, shoving it into her arms, pushing her phone into her unresisting hands. "Get in the closet."

"What?" Peri looked around confused, as he pushed her toward the hall closet.

"Vivian's here," he said shutting the door in her face. Through the louvered wooden slats of the closet door, she could see Shark throwing on his jacket and grabbing his keys. He dashed to the front door and exited. Peri stood in the darkened closet next to the water heater and wondered what to do next. Seconds later the door was opened and Shark re-entered.

"Well, if you don't have something for me, then maybe I have something for you," she said, her voice husky. Vivian kissed him, pressing herself against him. Inside the closet, Peri found her hand clenched around her phone so hard that she heard the case creak in protest. As she watched, Shark disengaged her hands and pushed her off.

"Not exactly in the mood, Viv," he said, using a clipped tone that she'd never heard from him before.

"So get in the mood," she snapped.

"I'm here to talk to Marko and then I'm heading out," he said. "I don't have time for this."

Vivian stepped back, her eyes narrowed in anger. "I'm tired of getting nothing but push back from you. You need to think about your priorities, or I'll be thinking about mine."

Vivian turned around and walked out, slamming the door.

Peri counted to ten and then ten again. Then Shark opened the closet. Peri pushed past him, making for the front door.

"Peri," he said, grabbing her arm. "Peri, stop."

"No," she said, spinning around. "I'm leaving. I literally don't like being in the closet."

"Peri, let's talk about this."

"There's nothing to talk about. I thought I could be all mature about this. I thought I could handle it. But I can't. OK? I can't. I can smell her perfume on you. Seeing her touch you, I just want to," her hands folded the air in front of her, "break all of her fingers."

He looked shocked and then furious. "And how do you think I feel about Trey?" he demanded.

"He's not even in the state!"

"Every time you answer one of his texts in front of me. Every time you pick up one of his calls when you're talking to me. You want a say in who I'm sleeping with then maybe you shouldn't be with someone else."

Peri stared at him, open-mouthed. Her only thought was that she owed Regan an apology. The drill team captain had been totally correct—Shark was jealous of Trey. Peri didn't know what to do with that. How was she supposed to react? What did Shark expect?

"Are you saying you want me to break up with him?"

"Yes!"

Peri felt herself break out in a sweat. Break up with Trey? Stop talking to him? Single status on Facebook? What about Christmas? Who would she talk to? Who would remember Vicki?

The lights in the room seemed to be narrowing down to just Shark's face. Her bag and phone clattered to the floor.

"No," she said, gasping for air.

"What? What do you mean, no?" He looked surprised.

Peri felt hot and clammy at the same time. "I need to go puke," she said and ran for the bathroom. Slamming and locking the door, she grabbed the sink for support as the tile beneath her feet spun. She was panting, but didn't seem to be getting enough oxygen.

Shark knocked on the door. "Peri, open the door." He sounded completely calm.

"No, this is embarrassing. Go away."

"Peri, sit down and put your head between your knees. Concentrate on taking deep breaths."

She thought about going to the toilet, but wasn't really sure she could make it. Instead, she bent over and rested her forehead against the cool marble edge of the counter.

Moments later, Shark walked in.

"I locked the door," she said. All she could see was his feet and legs and the broad tiles of the bathroom floor, which at least had stabilized.

"I picked the lock," he replied. "Deep breaths." He pulled out a washcloth and ran it under the shower.

"What's wrong with me?" she moaned, forcing herself to expand her lungs and take in air.

"You're having a panic attack," he said, ringing out the washcloth.

"How would you know?" she demanded.

"I knew this one guy—did totally fine in prison—got out and started having panic attacks. Outside life was really overwhelming for him. Your body goes into fight or flight syndrome without actually being in danger. You feel trapped, and your system gets hit with a massive dose of adrenaline."

Peri thought about this while taking in more air. The nauseous feeling was fading, but she felt shaky. Adrenaline dump would explain that.

He pushed her hair off her neck and put the damp cloth on it. She kept her eyes closed as he continued to stroke her hair. She felt her body starting to relax.

She knew the second he'd found the scar. His hand stopped moving on her hair. He didn't pull away. He just stopped moving.

"Don't look at that," she said, and her voice sounded harsh even to her own ears. She'd looked at it thousands of times in the mirror. It looked like a power button or a capital Q, but the part of the line inside the circle curled around to make another circle. It was about the size of a quarter and placed just behind her right ear, and she hated it every day as she combed her hair over it.

"OK," he said, pushing her hair back over the mark behind her ear. "But later, you're going to have to tell me about it."

"No," said Peri, twisting her head to the side so that he couldn't see the brand.

"Yes," he said, leaning down so that his face was on the counter next to hers and he could look into her eyes. "Because I'm going to need to know who to kill."

She smiled at him. "How do you always know what to say?"

"It's easy," he said. "I just say what I'm thinking and then you laugh. But I'm not joking."

"I know, but it doesn't matter," she said. "They're already dead."

"What happened?" he asked. His voice was gentle, like he didn't want to startle her.

She took the washcloth off her neck and dropped it in the sink. She went out to the bedroom and sat down on the bed. She'd never told anyone before. The closest she'd ever come was Al, and even then, she'd never given the real story. Would Shark care? Would he still want her if she told him? She wanted to believe he would.

"When I was thirteen, my best friend Vicki and I went to the mall. We took our mom's credit cards and we bought high heels and walked around the mall in them. Although, walking might be stretching the point. I must have looked like a giraffe. We thought we were so cool."

She stopped. She wished he would come closer. He was so much easier to read when she could touch him. In the bathroom, Shark picked up the washcloth and ran it under the hot water. He took off his shirt and tossed it in the general direction of the laundry hamper. On his back, she could see a trail of progressively larger sharks tattooed down his spine. He ran the washcloth over himself, scrubbing off the stink of Vivian's perfume. Then he gargled with mouthwash, rinsed, spit, and then came back to the doorway.

"We bumped into a guy she knew. He said he could get us some weed, so we followed him out to his van. There were other guys in the van. They grabbed us. I couldn't run in the stupid shoes. They drove us a long way and took us to a house we'd never seen. I suppose if you know what this is," she touched the brand behind her ear, "then you know what happened next."

He leaned against the doorframe between the bathroom and the bedroom, hands in his pockets, eyes on the floor. "They take your shoes, probably clothes. Inject you with whatever drugs they have on hand, brand you. Then usually they..." He trailed off. "Usually they rape you."

"In our case, it was meth. After they branded us, all I could smell was meat. We smelled like BBQ. I still can't eat BBQ, to tell the truth. The meth was kind of a relief, because it made the smell stop. They put us upstairs in separate rooms," said Peri, and she lifted her hand to her face, rubbing her nose and smelling the lotion on it. She let the comforting smell of gardenias push the memory of burning flesh away. "They handcuffed one of my hands to the bedframe. I don't know if you've ever done any meth, but apparently, it's pretty common to become sort of object fixated. It was one of those metal-frame Victorian beds, and what I remember is that I just kept spinning the piece of bedframe in my hand. At some point, the bed came apart, and I had a piece of metal pipe in my hand. It seemed like an eternity later— it could have been five minutes for all I know—a guy came in. He was already unbuttoning his pants. He wasn't even looking at me. And for some reason, that just pissed me off."

Shark had his face turned down. She couldn't see what he was thinking, but she went ahead with the rest of the story. It was too late to stop now.

"So I stood up on the bed and I hit him in the head with the piece of pipe from the bedframe. And I kept hitting him. I guess, at some point, he was dead. Unfortunately, they had taken the door handle off the inside of the door. I couldn't fucking get out. And I didn't know what to do. I tried to think about what my dad or Al would do. So I searched the body and I found a gun and I waited. It's possible that I passed out. Again, not really clear on the timeline. When I came to, I heard gunshots. Then someone coming upstairs and more gunshots. I stood behind the door and I waited. Someone came in, and he had a gun, so I shot him. I waited, but no one else came. So I went out, and I looked in the other rooms. I found Vicki. She'd been my best friend since we were five. She'd been shot in the chest, and they were all dead. Everyone. All the other girls. All the other men. Everyone was dead."

Peri stopped talking, blinking away the memory of the blood and the grotesque limp bodies. She'd never said any of this out loud before. When she'd tried to picture telling Trey or Al, even in her head, this was as far as she'd gotten.

"What happened next?" he asked.

"I went downstairs and I saw three other guys loading money into a bag." Her voice didn't sound like hers. She felt like she was listening to a recording of herself—hollow and tinny. "They didn't hear me. Probably because I didn't have any shoes on. I walked up behind one, and I shot him in the head. The other two started coming at me, and I just started shooting until there weren't any more bullets. I found my clothes and the high heels I'd bought at the mall, and I put the pipe and gun in the bag of money, and then I walked until I found a house with an unlocked back door. I went in, took a shower, used a hacksaw from the shed to get out of the handcuffs, stole some shoes, and walked to the nearest bus stop. I had to take a Greyhound back to town, and by the time I got back, it was time for school. I went through the entire day at school, and no one noticed that anything was wrong. That was when I realized that adults can't really see what's going on with kids. Trey was the only one who noticed Vicki was missing."

"What did you do with the gun and pipe?"

Leave it to Shark to always consider the practical aspects of crime.

"Don't worry, I managed my mischief. I wiped them down with nail polish remover and then dumped them in different parts of the river."

"Sorry, I forgot who I was talking to. Of course you did. You could have called the cops."

"Maybe," said Peri. "Maybe if I hadn't shot that guy in the back of the head."

"Self-defense," said Shark, shaking his head. "You were under extreme duress."

"Yeah, they always say it's OK for a girl to defend herself," said Peri. "But what they really mean is that it's OK to fight, as long as you lose. It's not OK for a girl to win." Shark looked like he wanted to argue. Probably because he didn't think like that.

"Anyway, it doesn't matter, because once I took the money, I couldn't call the cops. But I figured if I was going to be turned into a whore, then I'd fucking get paid. What I didn't realize at the time was that once I took the money, I couldn't help them find Vicki. It was two weeks before they identified Vicki's body. Her poor mom kept hoping she'd just run away. She put up posters everywhere. The worst part was that I helped her. Trey helped, too. He'd known Vicki just as long as I had. And I just..." she threw her hands up and let them fall back down to the bed. "I just kept my mouth shut. And the more I learned about what had happened to us, the more I realized that it wasn't just a few guys in a house—it was an entire organization. And then I realized that the cops weren't going to find the people who took us. Or maybe I should say, the cops weren't going to bother looking for the people who took us."

"So you decided you would find them?" asked Shark.

"Yes."

She stood up and rubbed her hands along her arms. Her fingers were icy cold, and touching herself raised goosebumps on her arms. "Yes." He was being so calm. She wished he'd give some indication of what he thought. She felt so stuck. She had felt stuck since that day. All her efforts had only been so much thrashing as the ice closed in around her, isolating her further and further from everyone else.

"I'm guessing you didn't tell Al?"

"He had just gotten out of the Marines. And, well, let's just say that at the time he was not the sober, gentle soul we all know and love today."

Shark snorted.

"Sometimes I think he guesses," she said. "But he never says."

"And you didn't tell Trey either?"

"No. I wanted to, but he's the only one I have left who remembers me from before. And I knew that if I told him, it would change how he looked at me and how he treated me. And it would become this thing, like a weight tied around everything. And now he's gone too. Because I killed his uncle."

"The Ukrainians killed his uncle," said Shark. "And in point of fact, it was Trey's mom who put the plan in motion. If we're going to blame someone, blame her."

"Blaming dead cancer victims is a bit hard to do," said Peri.

"I can do it, no problem," said Shark. He sounded angry. He walked over and put his arms around her, and she gingerly leaned into him, letting him hold her up just a little. Was it so bad to not stand on her own for a minute? She could feel his heartbeat against her chest. His skin felt fiery against hers.

"I'm sorry that happened to you," he said, holding her tighter. His voice sounded deeper with her ear on his chest. He was rocking her just a little, and his hand stroked down her back, and she felt herself begin to melt, breaking up into little pieces, drifting.

"Sometimes I think, if I had just done something differently,

Vicki would still be here." She had never come close to admitting that to anyone before. She could barely admit it to herself.

"No," said Shark. "None of that was your fault, and you're lucky—I'm lucky—that you made it out alive."

Peri felt her heart contract, spasming out of rhythm, as if she had been punched in the chest. She hadn't known it until he'd said the words, but she'd been waiting for someone to tell her that. Hearing him say it made her feel dizzyingly light. She looked up at him, unable to express the feeling that he'd lifted a weight off her shoulders. She rose up on her tiptoes to kiss him. His hands buried in her hair, and she let her hands run over his chest. The kiss went on far longer than she'd meant it to, shifting from gratitude to desire to passion.

They broke apart, and Shark held her face in his hands, staring at her in something like frustration. She waited.

"You don't have to break up with Trey," he said at last, grinding out the words. "For now, anyway. I'll deal with it."

Peri knew that the polite thing to do would be to say, *no, of course I'll break up with him.* Instead, all she could think was, *thank God, I don't have to make a decision.* She arched upward again, reaching for his lips. Her arms went around him, pulling him to her. She ran her hands down his spine, trying to find each of the sharks there by touch.

They sank onto the bed, and he helped her slide out of her shirt. His hands explored her skin, causing her heart to pound, but in a way far different than it had only a few minutes before. Everywhere he touched bloomed with warmth and heat, and she felt as if she were spinning upward. The feeling of floating continued even as they tangled together limbs, tongues, and hands. Maybe he was floating with her. She kicked off her shoes and reached for the buckle on his belt.

In the other room, her phone rang—Al's ringtone.

On top of the dresser, Shark's phone started to ring.

They stared at each other. It was like a crash landing.

"We could ignore them?" he suggested, but without a lot of hope in his voice.

"It's Al. He'll just keep calling until I respond. And if I don't, then he'll start looking for me."

"Mm," said Shark.

Both their phones stopped, and then, true to her prediction, her phone immediately began to ring again. His phone went ping with a text message.

He growled in frustration. "Fine, but we are coming back to this conversation."

"Trust me, the next person who gets between me and an orgasm is getting kicked in the teeth," she said, which made him laugh.

He stood up and then pulled her upright. She jumped into the pull a bit, so that she collided into him, allowing her to reach around and grope his butt. She enjoyed the surprise on his face and giggled as she headed for the living room, but not fast enough. He smacked her on the ass as she left, and she laughed at him over her shoulder.

"Hey, Al," she said, picking up the phone.

"You didn't answer," he said.

"I was peeing."

"Overshare," he said.

"Stop calling me when I'm peeing then."

"I drove by your house. Your mom's not home? Is she staying with Rodney?"

Peri checked her mental calendar. "Yeah, I think so. Why?"

"I figured we should probably regroup on the Happy Place situation. Was going to see if you wanted to crash at my place?"

Peri pulled the phone away from her ear and stared at it. Al never asked if she wanted to stay. If he was asking, would it look suspicious if she didn't go? How was she supposed to get out of this? She looked into the bedroom. Shark was on the phone and pulling on a fresh shirt, with jerky, furious motions. That meant she probably didn't have to get out of going to Al's.

"Uh, OK," she said, gloomily. Then realized what the call was really for. "You want me to bring you dinner."

"Since you're coming over anyway," he said, and she could hear the grin through the phone.

"Jackass," she said, shaking her head. "You want Thai or Mexican?"

"Surprise me."

"Yeah, all right. See you in a little bit then."

She hung up the phone, frowning. Still suspicious.

"Mine was Marko," said Shark, coming out of the bedroom. "He's on his way over. What did Al want?"

"Dinner, I think. He said I could crash at his place, though."

"Oh, good," said Shark, nodding.

"Yeah. Hey, I've been thinking about the guys in the U-Haul."

"When? In the thirty seconds between making out and talking to Al?"

"Yeah, in those thirty. You know what wasn't in their wallets or their pockets?"

"No, what?"

"Rental paperwork."

Shark scratched the scar on his eyebrow.

"If it's a real rentable U-Haul, then it should have rental paperwork and receipts. But they didn't. And who rents a U-Haul to do cash pick-ups? That's counter-productive."

"No one," he said. "Unless you don't have to rent."

"And why wouldn't you have to rent?" asked Peri. Their minds were clearly working on a parallel track.

"A U-Haul is relatively inconspicuous because they're so common. They can go anywhere. If I can have a bowling alley, then why couldn't the Scarecrow own a U-Haul franchise?"

"It's worth looking into," she said, with a smile.

Tuesday ~ March 14

Shark: Preston Peccary

Shark stood in Preston Peccary's lobby staring at more posters of the realtor. He was pretty sure the teeth were veneers. They looked too even. He looked around the office. The office felt the same way as the teeth—too shiny, too straight, too... perfect. He smiled at the receptionist, who smiled back. She was wearing almost appropriate business wear, but then paired her knee-length skirt and blouse with stripper heels. Also, he was pretty sure that the extra-wide band-aid on her forearm was covering the last phase of a tattoo removal. The ghosted marks on her skin looked like possibly the remains of *la familia*. Which meant that she was out of the Corazons—one of the all-Latino gangs that hadn't wanted Shark when he'd been shopping for a *familia* of his own.

"*¿Te gusta aquí?*" he asked.

"*Si,*" she replied with a smile. "Mr. Peccary doesn't like to work that hard, and neither do I."

"Who does?" he asked, and she laughed. "He likes that you're bilingual?"

"He speaks Spanish," she said with a shrug, implying that

Peccary had no need of her language services with the simple gesture. "His girlfriend is Latina."

Shark nodded.

"What about you?" she asked, batting her fake eyelashes at him. "Does your girlfriend know how to roll her R's right?"

Shark laughed. The receptionist had mastered innuendo level: expert. "Her Spanish is bad," he said. "But her sign language is great."

She made a skeptical face that managed to imply that hands could not compare with the joys of properly enunciated Spanish. Once again, he had the passing thought that if he had been with Francesca, he would have been suggesting that he and the receptionist spend a little time on the study of linguistics. But he wasn't with Francesca. And he *was* with Peri.

He'd tried pretending he wasn't. He'd tried pretending that it was a crush or a fantasy or the result of too much time in prison. Vivian was supposed to be the cure for all of that. But it hadn't worked. Nothing worked. Being with Peri felt like hitting the gas on a '69 Charger—everything just roared. Peri was everything he wanted—loyal, brilliant, fierce—and being with her made sense on a molecular level that he hadn't been able to articulate before now.

But now he got it. What Peri had been through... He knew what the therapists would say: trauma. But he knew that kind of trauma from the inside out. It could make or break a person. And when it came down to the moment of deciding whether or not to rise up or fall down, he and Peri had made the same choice. Knowing what had happened to her, it didn't matter to him, except that now he felt like he had a missing puzzle piece. It made everything make sense to him.

Of course, what didn't make sense was how quickly Marko had made him the previous evening. Marko had barely made it through the door before calling him out.

"You saw Peri, didn't you?"

Shark had tried to push back. "What makes you say that? Other than that, I said I'd talk to her."

"Shirt on the floor, and the bed is…" Marko leaned a little to look through the doorway into the bedroom, "in a somewhat distressed state, and you're…" Marko moved his hand in a watery motion in front of Shark, "relaxed and shit. She's like your human fucking valium. I don't know why you two can't figure it out. She's graduating soon—I asked Domingo. She could move into the city with you."

"Marko, if you don't want to be in the city because it's so fucking dangerous, then why would I want her there?"

"Maybe you could just sort of keep her out of sight?"

"You think I should do that to her?"

Marko's face was all the answer he needed.

Unfortunately, Marko's expression had also caused him to have serious doubts. When he had been kissing Peri goodbye, an extensive and enjoyable process, it had seemed so easy: get rid of Vivian, move Peri into her own place, take care of Geier, live happily ever after. Under the harsh light of critical thought, without Peri's skin, taste, smell, and body to distract him, it seemed a lot more complex.

There was a ping from the instant messenger on the

receptionist's computer, and she checked it. "Mr. Orcas?" she asked, eyeing him in disbelief. "Your name is Orcas?"

Ryan had thought he was fucking hilarious with that alias.

"My grandfather changed it from Jorcasitas," Shark improvised.

She immediately nodded. "Cool. Mr. Peccary can see you now."

He followed the receptionist down the hallway to an office. She held the door open for him. Preston Peccary sat behind an enormous wooden desk, beaming like his pictures. As Shark entered, Peccary stood up, and up, and up. What pictures had failed to capture was that forty-something Preston Peccary was at least six feet six inches tall, lanky and angular. Shark had to admit that if he were picking out someone to be Scarecrow Jack, Peccary fit the picture in his mind.

"Come in!" exclaimed Peccary, holding out a hand to shake. "It's so nice to meet you. Billy Orcas, right? Preston Peccary."

"Yes," said Shark, shaking the offered hand.

"Were you referred by someone, if you don't mind my asking?" Peccary gestured to a chair as he sat down again, and Shark took his own chair. Even sitting, it felt like Peccary towered over Shark. "I like to keep track of these things."

"No," said Shark, "but I can only drive by so many bus stops before I take the hint."

Peccary guffawed. "You've caught on to my marketing strategy. Nice to know it's working. What can I do for you today?"

"I'm interested in a condo. I'm new in town. Moved for my

job and since I'm going to be here a while, it seems like I should invest."

"Good idea, good idea," said Peccary, nodding. "Nice to see a young person with his head on straight. What are you looking for? If you don't know, that's fine too, we can visit some research properties."

Shark rattled off stats that were similar to his current apartment, and Preston nodded along. "You know this is a little unusual, but I actually have a property that might work for you. Do you have time? We could do a quick little drive-by and see if you like it. And that will give a jumping-off point to find you your dream home."

"Sure," said Shark, checking his watch. Through his eyelashes, he saw Peccary check out the watch and his shoes, probably estimating the price tags. "I work with the Hong Kong branch, so I don't have to be in the office for a few more hours. I think I've got time."

"Isn't that hard on the old body clock?" asked Peccary, standing up and leading the way out of the office.

"I self-medicate," said Shark.

Preston Peccary laughed in a way that was a little too knowing. "Haven't we all been there? Do you want to follow or ride with me?"

"Like I said, I'm new in town. If it weren't for map apps, I still wouldn't be here. Probably better if you drive."

"Great!" Preston Peccary flashed his smile again and led the way to a large gray Lexus SUV. Peccary took off his jacket and dropped it carefully in the back seat before climbing in.

"Hey, you know, I don't usually make the offer, but since you're new in town, let me know if you need any help in the medication department," said Peccary as he settled in. "I know it's hard to find someone reliable when you're new."

"Thanks. The guys at work keep offering," said Shark. "But honestly, their shit is shit. It's getting awkward."

Peccary laughed. "Right? You don't want to hurt their feelings, but at the same time, you don't really want to spend that much on baking soda?"

"Exactly," said Shark.

"Don't sweat it. I'll grab you something back at the office. If you like it, I'll give you my guy's number."

Peccary's driving habits were jumpy and erratic. Like many city drivers, he put speed as his highest priority, dive-bombing from opening to opening in traffic, angry at the other drivers blocking his path. Shark tried not to periodically pump the imaginary brake pedal on his side of the car, but it took a lot of restraint. They parked in the underground garage of a high-rise condo, and Peccary climbed out of the vehicle. Shark tried to assess how much of a threat the big man would be in a fight.

Shark's prison cellmate, a redhead with a foul temper named Chase Williams, had been an MMA fighter who'd been convicted for selling performance-enhancing drugs. Shark had always known how to fight. Punching people had never been a problem. What Chase had given him was an education on how to win and how to spot weaknesses in others. Shark considered it a tragedy that Chase had committed suicide before making it through his sentence. Chase would have made a good coach.

Shark applied Chase's lessons to Preston Peccary. Many big men relied on their reach and weight to simply grab and crush opponents, and the heavier they were, the more they had other health problems: stamina, weak knees, and speed. But Peccary was not heavy, and he moved briskly without looking inconvenienced by the effort. In short, Peccary looked like he might be a handful in a fight.

Peccary led him to a condo and opened the realtor's lock box on the door. Shark stepped inside and smiled. Jill Shapiro had clearly staged the apartment.

"Nice furniture," said Shark.

"Yeah, the owners used a staging company. It looks nice, doesn't it? If you like something, you can have it written into the deal or purchase it outright."

"Apparently, you can get me just about anything I want?" asked Shark, and Peccary laughed.

"I always say that my job really isn't about finding real estate, it's about meeting people's lifestyle needs."

"Good to know," said Shark.

"It's my general policy to have buyers wander around a little on their own," said Peccary. "That way, you don't have to feel like anyone's looking over your shoulder. But let me know if you have any questions."

Shark did as he was instructed. This was one of the moments when he wondered what normal people did. It was hard to act normal when he had no idea what normal was.

He stood in the bedroom and tried to picture himself living there. That seemed to be the wrong approach. He could live almost anywhere. He'd lived in a condemned house when he was fifteen to avoid foster care. Everything else seemed like a cake walk after that. Even prison had been a step up.

He knew that one of the reasons he liked expensive, well-designed furniture was because it signified stability. That no one would be shutting off the water. That there were no cockroaches or junkies to step on in the middle of the night. That no one would be coming through the door at three in the morning with a battering ram and a warrant. Of course, he also liked that it was just better fucking furniture than the pressboard pieces of crap that came in boxes and populated the rest of the apartments in the city.

He looked around the room again. It seemed nice? What was he supposed to say? How did people say no to perfectly nice apartments? As a last resort, he tried to picture Peri being there and then immediately dismissed the idea. The condo was loft style, and the bedroom had no doors—it was simply open from the stairs down to the main floor. If she didn't feel safe at her mom's, then this would be a definite thumbs down.

He went back down the stairs to the living room, where Preston Peccary was basking in the sunlight coming through the tall windows. He'd rolled up his sleeves and looked perfectly comfortable to wait as Shark nosed around.

"It's nice," said Shark. "I think everything looks good. But the bedroom not having any doors is a deal breaker for me. My girl won't like it."

"Well then, there's no point in even talking about it," said Peccary, grinning. "The female vote is all critical."

Shark smiled to signal amusement.

"It won't be a problem, though. I can think of at least three listings that are similar and have more enclosed bedrooms. Why don't I line up some showings for us in the next couple of days?"

"Sounds good," said Shark. He was starting to feel like he had wasted his afternoon. Most realtors probably had drugs on hand. It wasn't exactly the biggest of red flags. He needed something besides an offer of a coke connection and a creepy realtor vibe.

"Although," said Peccary, "I do like to get all the decision makers in the same room. Maybe your girlfriend should come along?"

Shark shrugged. "I like to take care of her, but she doesn't really get a vote. If you really wanted to meet my lifestyle needs, you'd tell me where to get reliable pussy. I only have the energy to cater to one woman. I want someone who knows when to leave."

"Always the hardest part, right?" asked Peccary, looking amused. "I've got a card back at the office. They'll take care of you. Age, weight, ethnicity. You can have whatever you want."

"I'd appreciate that," said Shark, trying to look genuine. "Glad I came in today. You're going to solve all my problems."

Peccary laughed again. "I'm here to help. Shall we head back to the office?" He gestured to the door. On the inside of his forearm, just below the edge of the folded back shirt-sleeve, was a scar. It looked a little like a Q with a second circle on the inside.

"That's a heck of a scar," said Shark.

If he killed Peccary now, he could probably get Jill Shapiro's stagers to take the body out for him. Wrap it up in one of those rugs in the dining room, take it down in the freight elevator. The floor, being hardwood, was a bit of a problem—that shit absorbed blood like crazy. Maybe get him over to the kitchen where it was tile?

"Oh, uh, yeah," said Peccary, folding his shirt sleeve down again.

But killing Preston wouldn't get him the rest of the organization, though. And Ryan knew where he was. Shark reluctantly let go of the plan.

"Camping incident when I was drunk and twenty. It was the end of one of those fancy marshmallow roasting sticks—it was supposed to keep the marshmallow from falling off. That was a joke. Burned the shit out of myself."

"Funny, isn't it?" asked Shark. "When you burn yourself like that, how it smells like BBQ?"

Shark: The Warehouse

Shark dialed Marko as he pulled away from the realtor's office.

"Good," said Marko, without preamble. "I was just about to call you.

"You've got something?" asked Shark. Last night, he and Marko had looked up every U-Haul company in a fifty-mile vicinity. They'd come up with three. One of them had to be the location they were looking for.

"I sent the boys to cruise the two that were closest to us last night. They said everything looked normal. And I know you said you were doing the one in the city, but I looked at the site online, and it looked small and not viable."

Shark grunted unhappily.

"Yeah, I know, but while I was looking at their website, I realized that they're promising rentals of full-size moving trucks, and there's no way they can store those on that site. So where are they getting them?"

"Good question," said Shark.

"Right, so I did some digging in public records. They have a storage site about twenty miles west of here, out in the boonies. But when you look at a map, that puts the bowling alley about halfway between them and Fowler's evidence warehouse. What you might term a natural meeting place."

"This is starting to sound promising," said Shark.

"That's what I was thinking," said Marko. "Eddie, Paper, and I were about to take a little cruise out there and do some recon. Do you want us to wait for you?"

"No," said Shark. "I have to check in with Geier. But call me as soon as you learn something."

"Got it."

Shark entered the warehouse to find Geier already two drinks in and pissed off. The anger wasn't unusual, but the drinks were. The Scarecrows were getting under Geier's skin.

Jill Shapiro was apparently drinking the green beer because the décor was rustic St. Patrick's Day with antiqued white furniture and green throw pillows on every surface. There was also a little dish of green M & M's on the bar cart.

On the other side of the room, as far from Geier as possible, Pompo sat nursing a fresh black eye. Devonte and Malone were lingering behind him. Malone looked like a worried puppy. Devonte was watching Shark with a tense, wary expression. It was hard luck when your boss was down.

"Where the fuck have you been?" Geier demanded as Shark sat down.

"Doing what you told me to do. Shaking down dealers and finding names."

"I told you to go with the others. Devonte says you've been cutting them out of the loop."

Shark looked at him—he was starting to think Geier had

wanted Devonte and the others to keep an eye on him. "I move faster on my own."

"Not fast enough," hissed Geier. "Crease is ahead of you."

Crease was indeed looking smug. Shark shrugged. "Great." Geier's eyes narrowed. Shark could tell that his refusal to be jealous of Crease was starting to bother Geier. Geier was only happy if everyone was at each other's throats. He couldn't tell what Crease thought about it.

There was an uncomfortable silence that Shark refused to jump into as Geier stared at him.

"So," said Crease, attempting to shift the focus back to himself. "I traced the weapons used in the hits last week to a dealer on the east side. After I asked him a few pointed questions, he said that the weapons weren't sold by him, but were direct from his supplier."

Crease nodded to the AV nerd who was back in attendance, and the TV flashed a picture of a white guy in a black leather jacket speaking into a cell phone in front of an apartment building.

"His supplier is a guy named Harry Johnson." There was the requisite snicker around the room.

Harry didn't look particularly tough, but the callouses on his knuckles said otherwise. Of course, with a name like Harry Johnson, that was what Shark would have expected.

"Johnson operates out of this apartment building on the East Side. I've investigated—Johnson occupies the first three floors, and above that is empty."

The AV nerd showed a picture of the building. It had a fresh coat of paint over some graffiti, and flowers—albeit sad droopy ones—in the planters out front. Someone was maintaining appearances.

"Do we think Dickface is the Scarecrow?" demanded Geier.

"It's unclear," said Crease. If he is, he's running the drugs out of a different location."

"They deliver direct to their dealers," said Shark. "No centralized clearing house."

"Where do they cut and package then?" demanded Geier, looking perplexed.

"I'm working on that," said Shark. "But it's pretty clear that they keep their people siloed."

"They're running them like terrorist cells," said Crease, nodding. "They keep each individual from knowing too much. That way, no one person can identify too many of their people. But it makes sense. Harry Johnson did two stints in the military, one of them in Afghanistan. That would give him drug connections and training. I don't know if he's the Scarecrow, but I'm certain he's who hit us."

"Then we can assume that it won't be easy to hit the apartment building," said Geier. "Suggestions? What's our plan?"

The room filled with chatter, and Shark turned to the AV nerd.

"What's your name?" he asked.

"Kyle Geier," he said, looking surprised. Shark ran that through what he knew about Geier. Geier had a sister, but the last time he'd bothered to keep tabs on the family, her kids had been… kids. Kyle looked like most of a fully formed adult.

Apparently, time hadn't stopped when he'd gone to prison, no matter how much he felt like it had for himself.

"Nephew?"

"Yeah."

"Scared shitless, yet?"

"Yeah," said Kyle, nodding.

"Hang in there. Just keep your mouth shut and you'll be fine. Meanwhile, can you look up the owner of that apartment building?"

Kyle frowned. "I've never done that before."

"There are a couple of sites online, or the county assessor's office sometimes allows searches."

Kyle began to type and, a few moments later, turned his screen to face Shark.

Shark grinned. "Thanks."

"What have you got?" asked Crease, coming over.

Shark debated how much to tell him. "I think Johnson's part of it, but I don't think he's the Scarecrow. I had a chat with a mid-level dealer up in Pomona Heights. He fingered a money guy. I think he's a better candidate for the role."

Crease nodded. "Who's the dealer? Can I talk to him? Maybe he'll know more about Johnson."

"Yeah…" said Shark. "He may have had a little accident."

"Shark," said Geier, looking relaxed for the first time in the meeting. Possibly Geier just fed off death and destruction. "I appreciate that you're so very tidy, but it does make it hard to question them again if they're dead."

Shark shrugged. "Sometimes you have to throw the little

fish back in the water. Or in this case, the pool. Plus, he was a junkie. Getting anything out of him was difficult at best. Look, I know you want to move, but I think we might want to wait a day. Give my guys a little more time to dig."

"Who do you think is the Scarecrow?" asked Geier.

Shark looked at Kyle, who turned the screen around to show Crease and Geier.

"Preston Peccary?" Crease looked skeptical. "The bus stop guy?"

"Who?" asked Geier.

"That's what I said," said Shark.

"Real estate agent," said Crease. "You know, he advertises on bus stops."

"Why would I look at bus stops?" asked Geier.

"Also, what I said," agreed Shark, earning an annoyed look from Crease. "But that's who my junkie dealer pointed to."

"It seems unlikely," said Geier.

"And he owns Johnson's building."

"Could be a coincidence. You got anything else?"

"Yes, but it's all sort of hearsay and instinct," said Shark. "I've got my guys digging for more."

"Your guys at the bowling alley?" asked Crease.

"They're just as good as anyone else's."

"Mmm," grunted Crease, stopping just short of a direct insult.

"We move tonight," said Geier. "If this real estate guy is part of it, then we'll have taken out his armory. If your guys come back with something else, we can move on that next. But right now, let's take out the known threat."

Shark could see that the decision had been made, so he nodded. Planning went well into the afternoon, and it was a long few hours until he could break free. He went back out to his car and ran through the texts from Marko. It was a series of U-Haul truck photos parked in a gravel lot. Two single-wide pre-fab houses sat further back on the property with an above-ground gas tank for fueling the trucks. Everything was surrounded by a chain link fence topped with barbed wire. Armed guards patrolled the grounds. There was a card reader at the front gate.

MOST SECURE U-HAUL LOT EVER. HAS TO BE OUR PLACE.

Shark sighed and texted back. WE'RE ON HOLD PER GEIER. WANTS TO HIT PLACE IN CITY FIRST.

Marko sent back angry emoticons.

AGREED. HOLD TIGHT.

Marko texted back almost immediately: BE CAREFUL.

Next, he started to text Peri and then realized everything was a lot more complicated than text. Finally, he settled for: CAN YOU TALK?

YES.

He dialed, and she picked up almost immediately.

"Hey," she said, and he could hear the smile in her voice.

"Hey. I need you to stay out of the city for the next twenty-four hours."

"Oh dear," she said. "You've moved to speaking in cryptic nonsense. This can't be good."

He laughed. "I've made some progress on Preston Peccary. I

think he's your guy. There's a U-Haul lot about twenty miles west of us. I think it's his base of operations, but I can't move on it. Geier wants to make a play on a location in the city first."

"That might spook him! And what if you all kill him first?"

"Then he'll be dead."

"Hey, I was here first. I have dibs. Tell him to step off."

"Oh yes, that's what I'll do. Excuse me, boss, do you mind not killing that guy? My girl has dibs."

She giggled. "Well, don't tell him. Just take him out of the way."

"Are you suggesting that I take over Geier's gang so that you can kill someone? And you call me weird."

"I was just throwing some suggestions out there. Creative problem solving."

"Well, the answer is no, for a variety of reasons, including that I would die."

Probably? He'd thought more than once about taking out Geier. He was fairly certain he could do it, but he hadn't actually considered straight taking over the gang. What would he want with The Organization? The Feds were about to crack it like a walnut—it would be worthless in a matter of months.

"Oh," she sounded put out. "Well, if you're not going to live through it, then there's really no point."

"Thanks. Look, we'll hit this place in the city, and then you and me, and Marko will make a plan for the U-Haul lot. It'll take some coordination. There are card readers at the gate. Guards. The works."

"Card readers?" she asked.

"Hey, someone's coming over. I'm about to ask you some inappropriate questions."

Malone, trailing Devonte, came over and tapped on the window.

Shark rolled it down as he spoke. "I don't know. What are you wearing?"

Malone leered. "Pompo wants to talk," he whispered.

Shark put the phone on mute. "Tell him to come outside. We can talk out here without Geier around." Malone nodded.

Shark unmuted the phone and held it back up to his ear as Malone walked away. The spring evening was chilly, and a mist was starting to creep in. He rolled the window back up.

"Problems?" she asked.

"No? Maybe. We'll see."

"Hm," she said. "Are you sure you shouldn't have Marko with you?"

He smiled. "You're not worried about me, are you?"

"I'm starting to have a vested interest," she said. "I'll be upset if you die."

"If I'm going to die, it won't be by Pompo," he said. "Meanwhile, what *are* you wearing?"

She giggled. "What do you think I'm wearing?" she asked.

"Uh, converse, tights, and a sweatshirt," he said.

"Ha! Shows how much you know. I just took my shoes off and I'm wearing a flannel, not a sweatshirt."

"Your phone sex is as good as your sexting," he said.

"I know! Not bad for my first time, huh?"

"What? I'm the first guy you ever sexted?"

"I broke the rules for you. Peregrine Hays company policy says sexting is a no," she said.

"Mine too, actually," said Shark. "So much opportunity for things to go badly."

"Why does no one else get this? Anyway, you're up to dirt tonight?"

"Yeah, so stay out of the city. And maybe you should stay away from Happy Place, too."

"Depends," she said. "If Angel puts out a call tomorrow, I'll have to go, or she might get suspicious. But yeah, I won't go into the city. You'll call me when you're done?"

"We're going early tomorrow morning. I won't be free until probably mid-afternoon."

He could tell by her silence that she wasn't pleased.

"I know I sounded like I was joking," she said, "but I was serious. If you're not going to live through it, then there's not much point in doing this."

"Don't worry. I know how to keep my head down," he said.

"I know that, but I still worry."

"You and Marko need to form a club."

"The Shark Takes Too Many Risks Club? I'm President. Marko's Treasurer."

He grinned. "Hang tight. I'll call you as soon as I can."

Shark: Pompo & Devonte

Shark saw Pompo come out of the Warehouse and look around nervously. Malone and Devonte were loitering by the door. Shark got out to meet Pompo in the parking lot because that was polite. Making the fat man get into his car would be an insult.

"Hey Pompo," said Shark.

"You took over the Reyes buy," said Pompo, his eyes looking flat and hard.

"Not on purpose," said Shark, "but yeah. You weren't there."

"I fucking got pulled in by ICE," he said.

"By ICE?" Shark was legitimately surprised. "I thought you had papers?"

"I don't need papers. I was born in fucking Cincinnati. I'm a fucking American, same as you."

"Actually, I'm not really sure about that," said Shark with a shrug. "Grandma knew some good forgers."

Pompo snorted. "Whatever, my point is, it was a dodge. Someone was rattling my can to see what shook loose. ICE didn't give a shit about me. They barely even questioned me. Some blonde bitch from the FBI took a couple of swings, but other than that, nothing. Once Devonte rounded up my lawyer, I was out in forty-eight hours."

"Have you told this to Geier?" asked Shark, wondering why Pompo was telling it to him.

"I gave him the outlines," said Pompo, "but I don't think he's getting the full import of what I'm saying. He's just pissed because I wasn't there. He's not hearing me. I'm telling you, the Feds are up in our business."

"Do you think they have anything on us?" asked Shark.

"I think if they had something, they would have moved. But I think if they hauled me in, then they're doing something," said Pompo.

"I follow your logic," said Shark, "but why tell me?"

"Because you can talk to the old bastard," said Pompo.

"You mean I can talk to him without getting shot," said Shark.

"Exactly," said Pompo with a grin. "I'm telling you, kid, I'm fucking worried about this and not because they threatened to deport me to fucking wherever the fuck I'm not from."

"Ohio?"

"God, that would be even worse," said Pompo.

"Do you think we should cancel tonight's action? Because I have to say without a smoking gun, he's not going to."

"No," said Pompo, "I don't think we're there. I'm just saying… someone needs to talk some sense into him."

Shark frowned. "It won't be tonight. He's too riled. He'd shoot his fucking sister if she tried to steer the ship right now. After tonight, we can try it again. Do it some place where he's relaxed, like Kos."

Pompo heaved a sigh and nodded. Then he stared at Shark,

suddenly angry again. "I'm still fucking pissed at you about the Reyes buy," he said, poking Shark in the chest. But Shark could tell there wasn't much behind it.

"What can I say?" said Shark with a shrug. "I'm good at taking drugs too."

"Yeah," said Pompo with a sigh. "I talked to Jesús. He said you went all tarot on 'em. I can't compete with that shit. I'm a fucking Buddhist." He shook his head. "Heading back in?"

"Yeah," said Shark, and then hesitated. "No. I was going to grab some extra ammo from the car. Meet you in there."

"Yeah," said Pompo, nodding and ambling away.

Shark went back to his car and popped the trunk. He pulled away the carpet to expose the spare tire and the three guns he kept with it.

"I know it was you," said Devonte, and Shark didn't turn around, but continued to reach for his guns.

"Know what was me?" he asked.

There was a clacking of a slide being racked on a pistol, and Shark finally looked over his shoulder. Devonte was holding a gun, but it wasn't pointed at him. Yet. "I know some people in the burbs. I heard a good rumor about you fucking your PO. It's the kind of story that spreads, if you know what I mean."

"Sure," said Shark. "No one gossips like a wise guy."

"The description was pretty clear—tall, blonde, tits for days, wears stilettos everywhere."

"What's your point?" asked Shark.

"Funny, but that's the exact description of the FBI agent that interviewed Pompo," said Devonte. "Which makes a lot more sense than a PO. What PO wears stilettos all day?"

Shark refrained from saying that he'd told Vivian that on more than one occasion. In fact, he didn't say anything.

"The way I figure it, you're working with the FBI," said Devonte.

"That's the way you figure it? Based off Pompo's description of a hot blonde?" He tried to look as derisive as he should have.

"I don't have to be right," said Devonte, "I just have to say it in there," he jerked his head at the warehouse, "and you're screwed."

The gun still wasn't pointed at him. Devonte wasn't angry. This wasn't retribution for Pompo, and it certainly wasn't loyalty to Geier. This was something else.

"What do you want, Devonte?" asked Shark.

"I want out. I can see the writing on the wall. Geier is bat shit crazy, and he's the kind of crazy that takes out everyone around him sooner or later. And that's not going to be me. You got a bonus for the Reyes thing. I figure you're the kind of guy who has retirement plans. I want whatever cash you've got, and then I'll blow town."

Shark thought about that. He was sympathetic to the cause—after all, that's what he was attempting to do—but he wasn't about to hand over shit to Devonte.

"I've only got like ten grand at the apartment," said Shark. "Everything else is in a bank."

"Bullshit," said Devonte. "You have a whole bowling alley

and crew of your own. I know you can get more cash than that. I want at least fifty." Devonte's gun came up.

"I don't have it lying around in the couch cushions," said Shark.

"I want fifty," said Devonte, reaching into his pocket and holding up a business card. "That FBI agent gave Pompo a card. He tossed it, but I picked it up. Maybe I won't start by telling Geier. Maybe I'll call hot blonde FBI agent Vivian Flood and tell her who you've been fucking around with at the clubs. I think she'd be pretty interested to toss your phone and go have a chat with Miss Digits."

"You think an FBI agent is going to give a shit about some girl at a club?" asked Shark, sorting through his options, and trying not to look like he was sweating.

In response, Devonte pocketed the business card and took out his phone. He flipped open the photos and held it out. The first was a picture of Peri kissing him, and the next was a full-face shot of Peri walking away. The colors were dark and garish from the club lighting, but Shark knew that Vivian would recognize her. Their encounter at the bowling alley hadn't been long, but it had been enough. Vivian would remember Peri, and she would not be pleased.

"I don't know," said Devonte. "Let's text her and find out."

"I have ten at the condo and I can get more, but not until tomorrow," said Shark.

"Then you've got until tomorrow," said Devonte with a smirk. He tucked the gun and card away and turned to leave. Shark reached out and wrapped an arm around Devonte's throat, dragging him backwards. Devonte clutched at Shark's arm, kicking out his feet, trying to lever his way out.

Shark threw him half into the trunk and brought the lid down hard on Devonte's chest. He heard the crunch of ribs breaking. He brought the lid back up and punched Devonte three times in quick succession. Devonte reached for one of the guns in the wheel well. Shark pulled the gun out of Devonte's waistband and struck him on the back of the head. Devonte sagged, unconscious. Shark looked around the parking lot. No one appeared to be watching them. He looked back at Devonte and worked through the angles.

He couldn't use a gun—it would be heard in the warehouse.

He couldn't turn Devonte into the FBI. Vivian could *not* have even a hint about Peri.

He couldn't have Devonte talking to Geier or Pompo.

Reluctantly, he pulled Devonte further out of the car, resting his neck on the edge of the trunk, and then, with a deep breath, he slammed the trunk lid down again. There was a sharp crack as Devonte's neck broke. Shark raised the lid and shoved Devonte all the way in. Then he took out the extra ammo he'd been looking for originally and tucked it into his pocket. He took Devonte's phone and deleted the photos, checked for a cloud storage app, and didn't find one. Devonte clearly didn't know to always back up his blackmail. Shark wiped the phone and tossed it back in Devonte's pocket, then he took out his own phone and checked his appearance in the camera. No blood anywhere. He smoothed his hair and dialed Marko.

"Hey," said Marko, sounding surprised.

"Hey," said Shark. "I need a little bit of help."

"Sure. What do you need?"

"After we all go out on the Harry Johnson thing tonight…" Shark paused while Marko smothered a giggle.

"Sorry. I can't help it. Who names their kid that? Anyway, yeah, after you all go out tonight. What do you want me to do?"

"I need you to swing by the warehouse and get rid of the body that's in my trunk."

"Oh," said Marko. "It's been one of *those* kinds of days."

"Yeah," said Shark. "And let's make sure it doesn't show up again anytime soon?"

"I bought extra cement last time," said Marko. "It's not a problem. I'll Mack the Knife him."

"Thanks, Marko. I appreciate it. I'll text you when we leave. Spare key is under the bumper."

"I'm buying myself a ninety-inch TV out of petty cash," said Marko. "And possibly a new fryer for the kitchen."

"Whatever you want," said Shark.

"Plus, a set of those super expensive chef knives," said Marko.

"I would assume top of the line," said Shark, heading back into the warehouse. "Although, how expensive are we talking? I saw one of those catalogs you were drooling over. The price tag was like five grand. That was just for one."

He walked through the shelves toward the center of the warehouse, pretending to be engrossed in his conversation, taking the opportunity to scout anyone who might be missing Devonte.

"That one isn't practical for what I want to do," said Marko. "I want a nice set that will hold up to repeated wear."

"This is going to cost me way more than five grand, isn't it?"

"Well, I don't know about exact prices. I'm just telling you my wish list."

Shark shook his head as he dropped down onto one of Geier's stupid Italian leather loveseats that fit no one and were never comfortable.

"Just try to keep your wish list within reason," said Shark.

"You got it, boss," said Marko, but Shark could hear him smiling through the phone.

"Talk to you later."

"Yeah," said Marko and clicked off.

Shark looked around the room. No one was looking at him except Kyle Geier, who smiled nervously. Geier was talking to Crease. Pompo was talking to Guetta. Malone was playing Candy Crush. No one seemed to notice Devonte was gone.

Shark: Harry Johnson's

Geier was having a blast. Literally. His weapon of choice was a shotgun, and he laughed every time he fired it. Shark followed along behind. He kept his head on a swivel and wondered if maybe putting one in the back of Geier's head might solve all the problems he currently had. Ryan would probably not agree.

The plan had gone well. Crease was a solid tactician. But it soon turned into a siege in one of the back bedrooms, which had been what Shark had predicted. Marko had already texted that the problem in his trunk had taken a swim. Everything was fine. No one needed him to do anything.

Bored, he returned to some of the front rooms, looking for anything that could tell him more. He was on the third floor in an open community room. The walls were now riddled with bullet holes. The big screen was never going to play again. One of the tall windows was open to a fire escape. The body of the last person who had tried to leave that way hung on the railing. Beneath the stairs, the back alley was an inky collage of black on black shapes, highlighted rather than illuminated by a single flickering bulb over the back entrance on the ground floor.

Three stories below the fire escape, bags of garbage had been mounded as they overflowed the dumpster. Shark turned to look at the room again. As he stared, he became aware of the sound of someone breathing. He crept toward a coffee table with a body draped over it. He upended the coffee table and the body at the same time, and a man came scurrying out like a cockroach.

Shark grabbed him by the collar as he scurried past and yanked him down to the floor.

"Hi," said Shark, looking down at a skinny guy with a three-day weed funk.

"Hi?" coughed the guy.

"What's your name?"

"Steve?"

"Are you asking me if your name is Steve?

"No? Please don't kill me."

"Do I look like I'm going to kill you?"

"Yes," said Steve.

Shark grinned. "Well, what if I didn't kill you?"

"I would really appreciate it?" Steve's eyes were so wide that there was white around the entire iris.

"But why wouldn't I kill you?" asked Shark, hauling Steve to his feet.

"Because you're a nice person?" suggested Steve.

Shark shook his head. "I'm really not. And you might want to try making statements." He heard movement from the hallway, and he began to walk Steve toward the open window.

"Statements? About what?"

"Well, Steve, what about a few statements on your organization? For instance, who's your boss?"

"Johnson?"

"That's good," said Shark, tapping Steve with the barrel of his gun in positive reinforcement.

"Please don't shoot me," said Steve again.

"Relax, relax, I'm not going to shoot you. Tell me about where the money goes. Tell me about Johnson and Peccary. Remember, I promised to let you go."

Shark was aware that the footsteps in the hallway had stopped. That was going to complicate his life.

"It's Peccary and Johnson and Javelina. They're the top three."

Shark nodded and maneuvered Steve to stand in front of the fire escape. He took out the phone Ryan had given him. "It's just those three?"

"I don't know. There might be someone else. Javelina was always talking about the reports and getting the reports right, but I never saw anyone else."

"And where are Javelina and Peccary now?"

"I don't know," said Steve.

Shark dialed Ryan and put the phone in Steve's pocket. "Don't move once you land," he said quietly.

"What?" Steve asked as Shark pushed him over the railing of the fire escape. Steve screamed convincingly as he went down. Shark watched him land on the pile of trash and roll onto the pavement. There was a twitch, and then Steve did as instructed and lay still.

Shark dusted off his hands and turned around to find Crease and Geier in the room.

"Oh. Hey."

"You said you were going to let him go," said Crease.

"I did," said Shark. "I let him go all the way."

Geier laughed and smacked Crease in the shoulder. "And you were worried that prison had made him soft."

Shark raised an eyebrow. "Because prison is so well known for that." In the distance, sirens began to wail. Shark checked his watch. "Response time in this area is two minutes. We should go."

They arrived down at the cars, and Pompo was arguing with Malone.

"I don't know where he is," hissed Malone, and Pompo slapped him on the side of the head.

"Problems?" asked Geier, startling Pompo and Malone.

"No," said Pompo.

"Malone?" asked Geier, enjoying watching Pompo twist.

"Devonte never showed," muttered Malone. "He went out to grab a burger and never came back."

Crease and Geier turned to look at Shark. He had a paralyzing moment of fear where he thought that they must know. But both Crease and Geier looked amused.

"Seriously, why the fuck am I the babysitter?" demanded Shark, hoping no one could see the sweat that had broken out along the back of his neck.

Geier laughed. "You're their age. I thought they might listen to you." Which meant that he'd thought it would be funny to annoy Shark with them.

"I can't make them grow brain cells," snapped Shark.

"Devonte probably just decided he didn't want to get shot at tonight. Can we go now, before the cops show up?"

Geier chuckled while Pompo and Malone glared at him, but no one protested as he opened the door to Geier's black SUV.

Shark rode in the back with Geier while Crease drove. Shark didn't like having other people drive, but he preferred this arrangement to having Geier sitting behind him with a shotgun.

"So where's the *I told you so*?" asked Geier when they were underway. "I heard what your little friend said. You were right. Preston Peccary is the guy."

"One of the guys," corrected Shark.

"Right. Any clue about who Javelina is?"

Shark shook his head. "I'll call Marko in a few hours. See what we've got."

"Well, remind them that we'll be handling it. I know you like to do things yourself, but I'm calling the shots on this one."

Shark nodded and checked his phone. It was nearly four in the morning. He wondered if he'd be able to ditch out for a few hours sleep. And how was he going to explain to Peri that Geier wanted to handle everything? She was not going to be pleased.

Wednesday ~ March 15

Peregrine: Surprise

Peri checked her phone. Shark's text this morning had not been reassuring. He'd said he'd call this afternoon, but it was now afternoon and he had yet to call. Her phone vibrated in her hand, and she hopefully checked the messages only to see the incoming text was from Javelina.

BIG SURPRISE! MEET AT THE CENTER ASAP.

She wasn't sure what to make of that message or the three emoticons of hearts and flowers that went with it. Emma texted next.

ALLY AND CARISSA ARE GOING. THEY SAY I HAVE TO GO TOO. ARE YOU?

Peri sighed. Big surprises from a sex trafficking, child porn pedaling pervert and drug dealer weren't really something she wanted.

YEAH, SEE YOU IN A FEW.

She checked her knife. Then she texted Al that she was going to swing by the center and got in the car. She wished she could call Shark.

She felt a chill of unease as she pulled up to Happy Place.

The parking lot was mostly empty except for a gray Lexus SUV parked in front. As she watched, other kids pulled in and parked. Peri followed them in. There were ten girls. She mentally checked them against her list. They were all Javelina's special kids.

"Hi, girls!" exclaimed Javelina as they came in. "Head back to the kitchen." Peri eyed the director. Her usually perfect curls were pulled back into a ponytail tail and instead of khakis and a button-up up she was wearing black leggings and a trim puffer jacket over a long sweatshirt. It made her look younger, harder, and a lot less friendly.

The girls chattered as they walked back to the kitchen. Peri began to assess her options. She could make a break for it. But that would mean that she might never find Scarecrow Jack, and it would also mean that the rest of the girls were on their own. She shifted her phone into the front of her pants, under her shirt.

How bad did she want this? How much was revenge worth?

The girls went into the kitchen, their voices echoing off the industrial appliances and tile. Peri followed, last in the herd.

"Just put your bags on the counter," said Javelina, coming in and closing the door behind her. The girls did as they were told and, like sheep who suddenly realized they were in the chute to the killing floor, they began to look around nervously. Two men opened a door to a loading bay, cold air blew in, and they all shivered. The men were carrying guns. Some of the girls screamed.

Angel took a pistol out from under her sweatshirt and held it in front of her. "Girls, try not to worry. Everything is going to be fine. I just need you to all follow these two gentlemen out to the loading bay and get in the truck."

"Why?" asked Ally.

"You said it would be a surprise," said Carissa.

"And isn't this a surprise?" replied Angel. "Get in the truck."

"No," said Ally. One of the men stepped forward and back-handed her. The rest of the girls gasped in horror.

"Get in the truck, or you'll be put in the truck."

Carissa helped Ally up, and everyone began to shuffle outside. They were pushed into the back of a U-Haul truck.

"Hand over your phones," demanded the man who had struck Ally.

Girls handed over their phones until at last he pointed at Peri.

"It's in my bag," she said. He stepped toward her menacingly, and she forced herself to back down and look scared. "Really, it's in my bag."

"Everybody, sit down," he said. "And shut up."

He slammed the rolling door closed with a crash, and a couple of girls began to cry in the dark. Peri put her hand up to the wall of the truck and took a few deep breaths. She could do this. The wall of the truck vibrated as the engine started. This wasn't the same as last time. She wasn't thirteen. Things weren't going to go down the same way. She had trained for exactly this moment. She felt a sudden uprush of panic.

She had trained so that this moment wouldn't happen again.

She closed her eyes and took another breath, counting backward from ten. She opened her eyes and found that they had partially adjusted to the dark. The girls were pale lumps in the gloom. Most of them were crying. Peri wanted to scream at them to pull themselves together. Instead, she took out her phone. She couldn't carry ten crying girls. If she was going to get them all out of this, then it was time to call the cavalry.

She took out her phone and dialed Al. He didn't answer, so she dialed again and waited for the beep.

"Al, I'm in fucking trouble. We all are. Go to my room. Third unicorn from the left. Find Marko at the bowling alley. He'll call Shark. You're going to need—"

Carissa suddenly lunged forward and seized Peri's phone, attempting to pull it away. She yanked hard, just as the truck took a turn, and Peri staggered, trying to maintain her balance. And Carissa took the phone with her as she went sprawling. Then, in the dusk of the truck interior, Peri saw her phone launch out of Carissa's hand like a firefly and smash against the truck's interior wall.

Emma wobbled over, fighting the road movement, and picked up the remains. The rest of the girls groaned.

"Nice job," Emma said to Carissa.

"You should have called 911," yelled Carissa.

Peri sighed and said nothing. If she said anything, she might as well just punch Carissa and move on.

She sat down and waited for the truck to stop moving.

"What's going to happen?" whispered Emma, sitting down next to her.

"We're going to get where we're going and they're going to take our clothes and our shoes," said Peri.

"Oh," said Emma.

"After that, it depends on how quickly they want to move.

We're a lot to handle all at once, so they'll probably stash us somewhere and then take us out one at a time."

"To do what?" asked the girl on the other side of Emma.

"You don't kidnap ten underage girls for their conversation skills," said Peri. "They're selling us as sex slaves. So usually they start by drugging you and then raping you."

"That's not true," said Ally. "Miss Javelina wouldn't do that to us."

Peri didn't say anything.

"What are we going to do?" asked Emma.

"Well, we're going to fight," said Peri.

"They seem really tough," said Emma, shivering.

"Then we fight more," said Peri. "And if that doesn't work, then we fight harder."

"Don't listen to her," said Ally. "Someone will come for us."

When at last the truck stopped, Peri had safely secured her knife in her bra. She couldn't say it was totally unnoticeable, but she could only hope they wouldn't be looking that closely.

The door rolled up, and the girls blinked in the cold light of the March evening. The same two men were waiting for them, guns pointed at them. Two more came forward, guns slung around their bodies. They had black garbage bags in front of them.

"Take off your clothes," said one of the men.

Everyone looked at Peri. Peri looked at the four men. She was fast, but she wasn't faster than a bullet. And even if she made it, at least one of the girls was going to get shot. That wasn't an acceptable level of risk.

"Do it," she said, bending down to unlace her shoes.

She really hoped Al remembered to check his messages.

Shark: Kos

Shark walked out of Kos and took a deep breath. Every time he left Geier felt like he was getting out with his life.

Al came out of nowhere with a right cross. Shark bounced off the wall and punched back before he really knew what was happening or who had hit him. When he realized who it was, he tried to push away, but Al was locked onto his jacket collar.

"Where is she?" growled Al. Shark felt a shock of fear run down his spine. It must have shown in his face because Al dropped his hands and stepped back. "Oh Jesus, you don't know."

Shark heard the door open, and he did the first thing he could think of—he punched Al. Al staggered back, confusion in his face, but his guard popped up, ready to go again.

"Uh, you need some help, Shark?" asked Malone.

"Do I fucking look like I need help?" asked Shark.

"Um, no?" Malone clearly wasn't sure about what the proper course of action was.

"Then get back inside." Malone retreated, and Shark waited until the door closed. Then he walked forward and grabbed Al by the arm, half pushing him towards the car.

"What the fuck do you mean—*where is she?*" he demanded when they were out of earshot of the restaurant. "She is supposed to be with you."

Al tried to pull away. "I'll handle it."

"Like hell you will," said Shark. "Tell me what happened."

Al hesitated, then pulled out his phone. "She's supposed to text when she goes near the Happy Center or out on a job for them. She texted when she left, but then I had my phone on silent. I felt it buzz. I thought it was her return text. So I didn't check it right away."

Al hit play on his voicemail.

Al, I'm in fucking trouble. We all are. Go to my room. Third unicorn from the left. Find Marko at the bowling alley. He'll call Shark. You're going to need—

There was a burst of static, and the message ended.

Shark felt a prickle along his spine as he began to sweat. "What was in the unicorn?"

Al held up a white key card. "I don't know what it goes to."

"I do," said Shark. "I just don't know how she fucking does this shit." He was turning over the options in his mind. He took out his phone and dialed Ryan.

"Problem?" asked Ryan, picking up.

"If I have an address on Preston and the Scarecrow Jack organization, how long until you can mobilize?" asked Shark.

"We have to get warrants and put a team in motion," said Ryan. "At least four hours."

"Too long," said Shark, and hung up. Then he dialed Marko.

"Hey, Boss, what's the word?"

"You have the address on the U-Haul yard?"

"Yeah, I thought the city guys were handling it?"

"They have Peri. We're going in tonight. Keep the crew tight.

You, Beef, Eddie, Paper. Domingo can drive if we need him. Bring the gear and go get another U-Haul truck."

"They're never going to let us in without a keycard."

"We've got one," said Shark. "We're leaving now. Text the address and I'll meet you there."

"You got it," said Marko and hung up.

Al was watching him. "We're not bringing those guys?" he asked, pointing back at the restaurant.

"Those guys are evil fucking bastards."

"And the guys you just called aren't?"

"They're my evil fucking bastards and every single one of them owes Peri."

"Good enough," said Al. "I'll follow you."

"Your Bronco isn't going to keep up," said Shark.

"Not driving the Bronco," said Al, pointing to a motorcycle. It looked fast standing still. "It'll keep up."

"Follow me then."

Peregrine: Showdown

It was raining when the truck door opened again. Peri caught a brief glance of gravel ground before they were herded from the truck and into an uncompleted half of a pre-manufactured house—the kind that went driving down the freeway, destined to meet its other half on some piece of property far away. The building was up on cinderblocks, and one whole side was just plywood and peeling Tyvek. The girls were pushed and prodded along slippery, wet plywood floors, down a hall, and into a cramped room. The door to the room was slammed shut, and Peri heard a deadbolt slide into place. Several of the girls were crying. The girl next to Emma had curled down into a ball and was sniveling.

"Stop crying," said Emma, harshly. "You're not even full naked. You got to keep your undies and bra." There was a blubbed, indecipherable response about boobs. "They're just tits," snapped Emma. "Everybody has them."

Peri tried not to smile as she climbed up on a pile of boxes to look out a window high in the wall. The window looked out over a gravel lot. There was another single-wide building directly opposite. A large, above-ground gas tank was near it. U-Haul trucks loomed through the mist.

"What do we do?" Emma demanded as Peri climbed down.

"We get out of here," said Peri, surveying the room.

"Who died and made you queen?" demanded Carissa.

Peri turned around and looked Carissa up and down. "No one. You want to fight me for it?"

"What?" Carissa stepped back. She looked around for support. No one was offering it. Peri decided she could now ignore her.

"Who's wearing underwire?" she asked, looking around. The girls all exchanged horrified glances. "Come on. One of you is. I need the wire to pick the lock. Cough it up."

Ally looked around the room. "You in the Dream Angel," she said, pointing at a hapless blonde. "Hand it over."

The blonde slowly took off her bra and handed it over, cringing. Peri removed the underwire and handed it back.

"This is going to take me a minute," she said, starting to shape the wire into the right shapes. "Some of you go through those boxes and tell me what's inside them."

Emma immediately began to unpack. Peri concentrated on the deadbolt. It was a heavy lock, but a light door. She had no doubt that if she wanted, she could kick through the damn thing, but she was trying for subtle. By the time she had the lock turning over, Emma had emptied the boxes.

"It looks like junk. Just random receipts and papers," she said in disgust. "An empty cigarette carton. Three boxes of tampons and four water bottles full of what I can only assume to be chew spit. Which is foul. Who does that?"

Peri shrugged. "The same people who think it's OK to sell girls into sex slavery?"

"No excuse," said Emma.

Peri didn't have a response to that. "I'm going to go do a little recon. You guys stay here. Keep everyone calm, and I'll be back in a jiff," she said to Emma. Emma looked scared, but nodded firmly.

"You're leaving?" gasped one of the girls. "How do we know you'll come back?"

"I don't know," said a mousey brunette with optimistic green highlights that were fading to a sad mold color, "Maybe you shouldn't. Maybe we should wait for someone to come get us."

The rest of the room began to murmur similar sentiments. Even Emma began to look uncertain.

"No one is coming," said Peri. "That's why we were picked. Did any of you call 911, parents, anyone? And how many of your parents know where you went? How many are going to come looking for you if you don't call in within an hour?"

They all looked around the room—their faces said it all.

"Then no one is coming. If we want to get out of here, we have to do it ourselves."

She looked at Emma, who nodded. "I'll take care of it," said Emma. "Just hurry back."

Peri cracked the door. The hallway was empty. She slid out through the door and stood against the wall, listening. She slipped her knife out of her bra and into her hand, where it fit with a comforting feeling of familiarity and reassurance. A cold breeze was blowing from the direction they'd come in, and she could hear voices from that direction as well. She stepped across the hall and tried the door immediately opposite her. It led to a room with a single bed. The bed had a comforter on it and nothing else. The comforter looked as though it had not been washed in years. Two large windows in the wall showed a chain link fence about ten feet away, then woods. The top of the chain link fence had barbed wire pointing out.

Peri went back to the hall and crept toward the cold air and voices. She approached the front door of the building—it was wide open. Two men leaned against the posts of the covered porch, one was smoking cigarettes, the other was chewing and spitting into a recycled water bottle just like the ones in the boxes. She could see the two plastic garbage bags containing the girls' belongings had been dumped by the door, one inside and one outside.

She craned her neck to get a better look outside. Across a wide expanse of gravel, she could see the other half of the house. She was looking at the back door. It even had a cheerfully bright yellow screen door. Close to the other building was a large gas tank and pump, as though it was a gas station.

"One more loop?" suggested the man with the cigarette.

"Yeah," said his companion, arcing a glob of black spit into the gravel. "When do you think we can have one of those?" He jerked his thumb over his shoulder toward Peri and the girls.

"After Peccary gets here, probably," said the first man, with a shrug. "Got to have the drugs on hand. I think Javelina's lining up buyers. She wants to move them all quick after that shit in the city."

"Fucking Geier," said the man with the chew and spit again.

"First Fowler, now Johnson? The Organization is kicking our asses."

"Yeah, well, I said we should have just tackled them head-on, but the bosses think they're all smart and shit."

"Whatever," said the guy, tucking his chew bottle against the house and stepping off the porch. "You coming?"

"Yeah, yeah," said the other man, and stubbed out his cigarette.

Peri watched them walk away and, with infinite slowness, tugged the corner of the bag closest to her until it fell toward her. She dug through and pulled out a sweatshirt and a pair of shoes that fit. She thought about grabbing pants, but she didn't think she had time for the argument that was going to cause. Then she picked up the bag and hurried back to the room filled with Happy Place girls. She opened the door, and everyone gasped and then exhaled in relief.

"OK," said Peri. "I managed to get one bag. I can't get the other without being seen, so we're going to have to share." She pushed the bag over and everyone scrambled for clothes. When they were all semi clothed, they turned to her expectantly.

"Next we're going to go across the hall. But first I need you to empty out the chew bottles and stick a tampon in the top of each of them." There was an exchange of looks and silent argument until finally someone decided they were lowest on the totem pole.

The bottles with their tampon toppers were handed to Peri with shrinking fingers and disgusted faces. Peri tucked them under one arm then cracked the door, checked for guards, and stepped out.

She opened the door to the other room, then stood guard until all the girls were in the other room. When they were all in, she shut and re-locked the door so that everything looked unchanged from the outside.

"OK," she said, stepping into the second room.

"I don't see what good this does," complained Carissa.

"Well, we have clothes don't we?" snapped Emma.

"You can always go back," said Peri. "Up to you. Meanwhile, I think the rest of us would like to escape." She looked around the room and got nods from all the girls.

"OK, here's the plan. You're going to divide into groups of three. You're going to exit through these windows. You're going to take this blanket with you. The first group is going to be the best climbers. They're going to go up and put the blanket over the barbed wire. Then everyone else will follow. As each group climbs over they are going to start through the woods. You wait for your fucking group, is that understood? You don't have to wait for everyone, but you have to wait for your fucking group. Got it?"

There was a chorus of nods.

"OK, once in the woods, you run as straight as possible. If you run straight you will hit a road. Once on the road, you will take a left. There are houses and people to the left, so you have to go that way. Now which way do you go through the woods?"

"Straight," said Emma firmly.

"What way do you turn on the road?"

"Left," said the Dream Angel blonde.

"Good. Also, you flag down anyone in a car that you can. Make them call 911."

"They're going to spot us," said Carissa. "If anyone comes around the house, they'll see us."

"I'll take care of that," said Peri.

"How?" demanded Ally.

"I'm going to cause a distraction. Now, which one of you got your watch back?" A dark haired girl who'd netted pants and shoes raised her hand.

"Great. Give me four minutes and then start group one."

"This is crazy," said Carissa. "You can't go out there. They're going to kill you."

"People always say that," said Peri. "But it hasn't happened yet. Ready?" She pointed to the dark haired girl with the watch who nodded. "Go."

Peri stepped out into the hallway again and gently closed the door.

How long since she had called Al?

She looked at the slowly molding drywall in the hall and tried not to be scared. Tried not to think that this shitty house would be the last thing she saw.

Was Al looking for her yet? Would he call Shark?

The fear was all around her in the hall, looming there over her shoulder, plucking at the sleeve of the sweatshirt that wasn't hers, trying to make her feel shame for her naked legs and basic granny panties.

But that was what *they* wanted. They wanted her small,

humiliated and fearful. They wanted to take the power of choice away from her. No one got to do that. The choice was always hers—starting with the choice about what to feel.

But…

She still wanted Al. She really wanted Shark. She'd have happily taken Marko and Domingo. Hell, she'd even take Paper.

Peri shook her head. She had staked her reputation on being able to take care of business alone. That's why she didn't have a gang, right? First real challenge and she was going to start running to find a man to protect her?

She could do this. This was what she had trained for. She was not small. She was not ashamed. She was not afraid.

Peri squared her shoulders and in the gloomy dark of the hallway she smiled.

They were the ones who should be afraid.

She went back to the front door. A drizzling fog of a rain had settled in, and across the compound, lights were starting to come on.

Peri stepped out onto the covered porch and picked up the lighter and box of cigarettes from where the smoker had left them next to the ashtray. Then, sticking to the shadow of the house, she worked her way to the end of the building. She hesitated a long moment before sprinting across to the gas tank. Her heart was jack-hammering as she used the pump to fill her three empty bottles. She swiveled her head around like an owl, spilling gas on her fingers as she switched bottles.

The houses demarcated the sides of a large gravel square, and the ends were filled with equipment. One side was full of construction machines, the other side had U-Haul trucks and a road that led to the gate out of the compound. Peri tucked her head down, ignoring that road and the beckoning escape, and re-inserted the tampons into the tops of the bottles. She used the cigarette box to wedge the gas nozzle handle down—the gas came out in a gush—then pointed it toward the field of trucks, watching the pool spread out in little rivulets, a rainbow sheen distinguishing it from the rainwater. She added a few more punctures to the gas tank with her knife, the hard steel of her knife driving through the skin of the tank with surprising ease and a pleasing pong noise. Finally, she lit the tampon on one of the bottles and tucked it near the nozzle.

She ran to the middle of the square between the two house halves.

"Hey fucktards," she yelled. "Who wants to come out and play? Come on, big boys! Come out and plaaaaaaay!"

Three men came out of the yellow screen door. Two more came out of the truck yard. They all ran toward her. Peri put on speed and ran toward the line of back-hoes and equipment on the far side of the square. The men gave chase. She ducked down behind a Kobuta thing with claws just as her tampon-based Molotov cocktail ignited the gas tank. The explosion was deafening, and chunks of metal and fire rained down on the entire yard. She didn't see the fireball, but she saw the reflected light of it on the machine in front of her. Around her, the air turned to steam. There were screams from the men who had been chasing her. She began to laugh and then bit her lip, trying to stop herself, even as her shoulders quaked in mirth. She really hadn't expect-ed the explosion to be that big.

Peri risked a glance out into the open space between the houses. More men were coming out of the second house, heading for the one that had housed the girls. From her vantage point, she couldn't see if the girls had made it over the fence yet, but she knew they would need more time.

Peri lit the tampon on the second gas-filled bottle and stepped out into view. The gas tank was a black flower of split metal, and it billowed black smoke skyward into the gray rain. It was still burning at the center and in a long trail toward the U-Haul trucks. The air was hot and reeked of gasoline.

"Hey assholes!" she yelled. She had to yell again, louder, to be heard over the sound of the fire and the cursing of the men across the yard. Finally, someone heard her and motioned to the others. Like lemmings, they all switched directions at once and came at her.

Peri threw the bottle at the approaching men and ran away from the fence—toward the back of the second house. She glanced over her shoulder to check the carnage. Two men were on fire, and the others were stopping to put them out. She round-ed the corner—two more men charged at her from the opposite end of the house. She wondered how many were actually here. They yelled at her to stop. One fumbled for a gun that was slung around his body, the other reached out as if to block her.

Peri didn't slow down. Instead, she lowered her shoulder, hiding her knife with her body, and rammed the one reaching out for her in the stomach. He grabbed at her, but it was too late to stop their descent, and they slammed down into the dirt with a hard smack. His head hit the gravel, her knife buried in his chest. Peri spun around on his chest, using her knife as a pivot point, grabbed the gun on his hip, and shot upward at the other man. His eyes stared stupidly down at the bullet holes in his chest, his hands reaching vaguely in her direction, and then he slowly sank to the ground and was still.

Peri stood up, taking deep breaths, trying not to choke on the smoke-filled air, and wondered how far the other girls had gotten. She dismissed the thought. She didn't have time for thinking—she needed to keep moving. She bent down to retrieve her knife from the man's chest, noting the scrapes across her knees and legs, when she felt an impact on her left side. Her gun went flying as she and her assailant sprawled in an untidy heap on the ground. She could feel the grind of gravel on her un-protected skin as the man pushed her down. He was bigger than her, with meaty arms and an oppressive weight that was going to be hard to shake off. He reached for her neck, attempting a choke hold.

Choke holds, as Al had explained on more than one occa-sion, were more complicated to execute than the movies make them look. Her assailant's grip was unsecured, and he couldn't figure out how to apply pressure to a smaller neck like Peri's. He pulled her up to her knees, which was only a favor to her. She elbowed him in the stomach and did a sit out, levering his elbow off her head. She popped to her feet and kicked him in the face. She heard footsteps and looked for her next attacker, spinning even as the man sagged sideways, unconscious.

Angel rounded the corner with a knife in her hand and pulled up short, seeing Peri. Peri wiped blood away from her eye. She couldn't remember what had caused the injury, but it didn't matter.

"What the hell do you think you're doing?" Angel demanded.

Peri stepped forward. This was the prey she really wanted.

"We can talk about this, Peri," said Angel, stepping closer, but she looked uncertain.

"Can we, Angel?" asked Peri. "Can we talk about how you're killing kids? Can we talk about how you're selling children?"

"Don't be ridiculous," said Angel, her voice pitched to sweet and saccharine. "I care about all my kids."

"Like you cared about Lara?" asked Peri, her head cocking to one side, watching as Javelina inched closer.

"Of course I cared about Lara," said Angel, with a smile. She looked so sweet—if you ignored the knife in her hand. It was a fixed six-inch blade with a curved tip and a serrated back edge. It looked like military surplus. Al had something similar. Peri had practiced with it on multiple occasions.

"What happened to her was a tragedy," continued Angel, sneaking another little bit closer. "It was very upsetting. But that doesn't have to happen to you. I can help you."

"And who's going to help you?" asked Peri, grinning as Angel stepped within striking distance.

Angel's smile dropped away, and she snaked forward, stabbing at Peri. Peri pivoted left, blocking with one hand, grabbing the older woman's wrist with the other, before turning back, cranking the arm until the knife folded back toward Angel's face. Angel screamed and dropped the knife as Peri applied more torque to her wrist. Peri released her hold and slammed her elbow into the other woman's cheekbone.

Angel staggered back, and Peri scooped up Angel's knife, hefting it in her hand. She didn't like it—the blade was too long and awkward, but it would have to do for the moment. Angel, her hand on her face, stared at Peri, eyes round in fear. Then she turned and ran back along the house. Peri followed, ducking through the door after the older woman.

Angel ran through the kitchen, throwing everything within reach at Peri as she went. Then she sped down a hall. Peri watched her slam through a door and out into a large open room with a few scattered boxes.

"What do you want?" she screamed as Peri came in after her.

"I want you to die in pain and fear," said Peri, with a smile.

The answer seemed to steady Angel more than a lie or an attempt to negotiate. She rounded on Peri, her guard came up, and she kicked out. Peri blocked the kick and sliced outward with Angel's knife. It slid along Angel's arm with the small satisfying sense of resistance that told Peri she'd connected. Another kick and punch. Another block and slice. Angel was dripping blood and panting.

"You're going to pay for this. He's going to kill you." Angel hissed and swung again.

Peri saw her opening, closed the distance, and stabbed Angel up under her ribs. Peri heard a popping in the distance, but she couldn't focus on anything but Angel's face—it was frozen in the shock of death.

"He can try," she said as Angel fell away from her.

In her peripheral vision, she caught a blur of movement. She tried to slip the incoming punch, but she knew it was too late.

The punch, when it landed, lifted her off her feet and sent her flying.

Peri looked up from the ground and shook her head, trying to clear the stars from her vision. She clutched convulsively for the knife and wished it were her own. When she was finally able to see straight, she saw Preston Peccary kneeling over Angel's body.

"Angel! Angel!" He shook what was left of Roseangel Javelina, but she was gone. "What the fuck did you do?" he whispered, turning to look at Peri.

Peri laughed as she climbed to her feet. It was a nervous reaction that she could never seem to stop, even though she knew it pissed people off. Al could show up any time now. She'd be OK with that.

"What's the matter?" she demanded. "Did I take away someone you love?"

Preston Peccary pulled himself upright, and for the first time, she saw his full size. He towered over her. He'd tower over most everyone. Behind him, she saw two men drag Emma, Ally, and Carissa into the room. Emma had a bloody nose, and the men had machine guns slung across their bodies. The girls looked terrified. She couldn't blame them. Things had officially gone in the shitter. On the other hand, they had been the last group. Hopefully, the other girls had made it at least to the road. There was a chance that help was on the way. She just had to stall.

She took another look at the girls. Ally was sobbing, and Carissa was holding her side and looked ready to fall over. Peri didn't think that she was going to get any help there.

"You're going to die," Preston said. "Do you understand that yet? You're going to die here. I'm going to kill you."

Peri could see that he was serious. She could see that he out-weighed her, and his arms looked practically the length of her body. She could see that he had back-up, and she was alone.

None of that meant that he got to see her fear.

"I've heard that before," said Peri. "It's getting boring. How about this one? I'm going to kill you like I killed your bitch."

He charged at her, reaching out with his long arms. She almost avoided. He caught a piece of her sweatshirt, swinging her back around to him. She sliced upward with her knife, cutting through his suit jacket as he punched out into her gut.

She staggered back and knew he'd taken her wind. She also knew that there was a split second of air left between standing up and lying on the floor, gasping. She used that second to run forward—ducked under Preston's hands, sliced at his ribs, and punched with her other hand.

Peri kept running, but his first punch finally caught up with her. She sucked in air, wanting to double over and stop. Instead, she pushed forward, her lungs burning, her body folding in on itself even as she demanded it keep moving. He chased her, and when she felt his hand on her shoulder, she dropped down to the floor and curled into a ball. It was a relief to stop trying to force her body forward.

Preston stumbled over her, tripping and going down onto

one knee. Peri tried to spring upward and knew even as she did so that she wasn't going to be fast enough. Her knife stuck into the meat of the tall man's shoulder as his giant hands locked around her neck.

Peri rammed her elbow down onto Preston's wrist, but his hold didn't break. She tried again, and he laughed.

"What are you doing, little girl?" Preston Peccary demanded, squeezing his hands tighter around her throat. "Are you trying to fight? You're going to die here. No one cares about you. No one is coming to get you."

There were sparkles around the edges of her vision. She was going to pass out soon.

Maybe he was right.

But who gave a shit if he was right?

Fight.

She kicked out, aiming for his balls. He blocked with his knee, but his grip loosened for a fraction of a second, and she sucked in air even as he shoved her to the floor.

Fight more.

Peri's eyes searched the space around her desperately. There was a wire hanger on the floor to her right, and she reached for it, stretching her arm out as far as it could go. He shook her and dropped to his knees, banging her head against the plywood floor. In the distance somewhere, she could hear yelling. There was the sound of something splintering, but that might have been her imagination, and all she could really hear was the sound of her own heartbeat pounding in her ears like waves.

Fight harder.

"What the hell is that?" Preston snarled to his men and looked over his shoulder.

Peri's fingers snagged the wire hanger, and she slid it further into her grip and whipped it across his face. Preston roared in anger and threw her across the room like a rag doll. She landed against some of the stacked boxes, feeling the hard corners crunch into her ribs and spine. She flopped forward onto her face and tried to push up. He was coming toward her again. She needed to move faster, but all she could do was try to inhale. Across the room, she could see the girls clinging to each other, watching her with horrified eyes. The gunmen were barely looking at the three girls. Instead, they were watching Preston—one of them was smiling, anticipating Peri's death. Any of the girls could have made a move. They could fight, but they weren't going to. No help there. As usual, Peri was on her own.

There was another splintering sound—unmistakable this time.

"What the hell is that?" demanded Peccary, pivoting back toward the door.

There was more yelling, and then the unmistakable sound of gunfire.

"That," said Peri, her words coming out in a wheezing cough, "is someone coming to get me."

The back wall of the house exploded in a shower of wood and glass as it ripped away. Through the gaping hole in the side of the house, Peri could see Marko sitting in the seat of a backhoe, grinning at his destruction. At the same time, the door was kicked in, and Shark and Al stepped into the room.

Peri usually thought that when committing acts of violence, Shark looked thoughtful, as if he were a master painter contemplating where to put the next brushstroke. She had never seen this Shark before. His face was contorted into a snarl of rage, and every part of him seemed flexed and taut. It occurred to her that this was the first time she'd ever seen him truly angry.

Shark raised his gun toward Preston, saw that the slide was back, the magazine was empty, and tossed the weapon away before charging the taller man. The two men holding onto Emma, Ally, and Carissa began to move, raising their guns, but as the one holding Emma let go, she clawed at his face. Distracted, neither man saw Al enter directly after Shark. The guard slapped Emma and waved his gun at the other two. The other was already turning back toward Shark, but Al fired—two bullets, center mass for each of them—and they went down.

Shark closed with Preston Peccary, and Peri knew from the first strike that Peccary was in no way prepared to deal with the meat grinder that was Shark's fist. Each punch landed with a sound like the killing bolt in a slaughterhouse.

Peri thought she should help—at least get the girls out—and pushed herself upright. Which is when her world went white, sideways, and then dark.

"Peri!"

There was jostling and movement. And somewhere, someone was yelling.

"Peri. Peri baby, I really need you to wake up now." Shark was talking, but it seemed like from a million miles away. She tried to open her eyes, but only managed to twitch her hand.

Which seemed odd because that wasn't what she had been trying for at all.

"Shark, we need to go now!" Marko sounded very tense. There was a high-pitched sound of sirens in the distance that was making it hard to concentrate.

There was a jolt as whoever was holding her shifted position.

"Then you go. I'm staying."

"No, we really need to go," said Marko.

"I'm fucking staying," Shark yelled. "Just go."

Peri didn't think she'd ever heard Shark yell at Marko before.

"Peri," said Shark, quieter now. "Peri baby, open your eyes." She finally managed to do as he asked. Her throat felt on fire, but the rest of her body seemed separated from her by a thick blanket. She blinked and tried to focus. Some distance away, Marko and Al were arguing, but silently, using all hand gestures. Al was pointing toward her and making chopping motions. She pulled her gaze further upward and found Shark's dark, fringed gray eyes staring down at her.

"There you are," he said, relief sweeping across his face.

"Hi," she said. Or at least she tried to say. Nothing came out. But it still made him smile.

In her peripheral vision, Marko was coming in their direction. He stepped up behind Shark, and his arm swung down. There was a thunk, and Shark slumped away from her. Peri opened her mouth to scream, but again, nothing came out. She tried to reach out to Shark, but her limbs were as cooperative as her voice. As she watched, Paper and Marko swung Shark up between the two of them and carried him out through the demolished side of the house.

Peri pushed herself upright and was trying to get her legs to function, but Al was already picking her up. She flailed against him, but he ignored her, carrying her the wrong way, in the opposite direction of where Shark was being taken.

Thursday ~ March 16

Shark: The Condo

Shark looked up as Marko came back from the door with Al in tow.

"I'm going to go get some coffee," said Marko, looking from one to the other, and edging away. Marko had spent a lot of the previous evening providing ice bags and standing just outside of arm's reach. Shark could have told him not to bother. At the moment, he couldn't have won a fight against Marko even if he wanted to. As far as Marko knew, he'd just kept Shark from getting his ass thrown back in jail. How was Shark supposed to be pissed about that? But this time, he suspected Marko just wanted out of the awkwardness of a parent-boyfriend conference. Al waited until the door closed behind Marko before saying anything.

"You look like shit," said Al.

"That happens when your friend hits you over the head with a gun," said Shark.

Al sat down in the chair opposite. "Also, when you try to punch your way through a giant motherfucker."

Shark shrugged. Bruised ribs and a couple of scuffs weren't that much to complain of. Geier had given him worse.

"You didn't come to my place the other day to rearrange my furniture and talk about Peri. You came for the photo of you and Vivian Flood."

"I needed it," said Shark. "Also, seriously, buy a fucking chair. No one has just a couch."

"You needed it to kick-start an Internal Affairs investigation into your FBI handler, right?"

Shark was annoyed. His head hurt and he was annoyed about, well, about everything, but at the moment it was that Al— Mr. Worst Computer Password Ever—had Shark dead to rights for the second time. Shark nodded. He wanted to add something cutting, but he really wasn't feeling up to clever right now.

"Yeah, that's what I figured. I've got FBI agents crawling over me like fucking lice, but none of them are asking the right questions, and they're telling me all the answers. Your friend Ryan Holden is running a cover-up. Apparently, I, in conjunction with a team of Bureau operatives, acting on intelligence I received during the course of my work, moved swiftly to save all the girls and stop a despicable group of sex traffickers. You were never there. Marko and your other friends were never there. I don't know how you're going to explain that to them, so good luck with that."

"I'll tell them that you pulled some strings," said Shark. "That you have leverage from when you were in the military."

Al shrugged. "Like I said, good luck."

"What about Peri?" asked Shark.

"Got interviewed as one of the girls, but other than that… Not getting mentioned. The scene is a fucking mess—bodies and blood everywhere—but so far they haven't noticed the knives I picked up. I think she might skate clean. Especially since they don't want anyone looking too hard while they clean up after you."

Shark nodded, relieved. Then he ran the angles again. "And because they want you to cooperate in the cover-up?"

"Yeah. That's the deal. They haven't said it out loud—suits never do—but I think Holden and I are clear."

"You have a lot of experience in the suit department?" asked Shark, narrowing his eyes.

"More than I'd like. You've been under since you got out of prison?"

Shark nodded again. "I cut a deal to get my record wiped. Fresh start if I can bring the Feds Geier. Which would have been a lot easier if my handler wasn't on the take."

"Does Peri know?"

Shark shook his head.

Al took a deep breath and let it out again slowly. "What the fuck is wrong with you two? Do you think you're invincible? Neither of you is fucking bulletproof."

Shark blinked. This wasn't the direction he'd expected Al to go. "We're OK," he protested.

Al stood up angrily. "You're not OK!" he bellowed. "You're on concussion protocol, and she can't fucking talk. I can see the damn fingerprints on her neck! You two think you're so clever that you can walk through this shit?"

"No," said Shark. "Yes." He wished Al would stop yelling. It was making his head pound. "I can handle it."

"Oh, you can handle it? Look around. You are in the deep end. I know you're swimming and you might even make it, but Peri doesn't need to be dragged down."

Shark stood up and then closed his eyes as the world swam a little in front of him. "Yeah," he said, grabbing the back of the chair. "I know."

Al scrubbed at his beard angrily. "You obviously care about her, and I'm sorry about that because it would be a lot easier if you didn't. But you can't see her again."

"I know," said Shark. "She's been on the news too much. If it wasn't Geier's guys, then Vivian would spot her. I can't have that."

"You and me both," said Al.

Friday ~ March 17
St. Patrick's Day

Peregrine: The End

"Maybe I should stay home today," said her mother. She was doing classy St. Patrick's Day with a green scarf, but she tugged nervously at it while staring at Peri.

"You stayed home yesterday," whispered Peri. "I'm only going to go back to bed."

Her mom looked at Al for back-up, which, considering their history of brutal sarcasm, snide comments, and occasional yelling when Al had been under the influence, was the weirdest thing Peri had seen lately. Al ignored the look and concentrated on the newspaper in front of him. "You're going to stay, though, right?" she asked.

Al could have pointed out that since the press were camped out in front of his apartment that their place was easier for him too. Al could have pointed out that he was expecting his lawyer and more FBI agents to arrive in a few hours. Not that he would tell Peri what the meeting was about. He could have pointed out that he'd already said he would stay—twice. But Al didn't say any of that.

"Yes," he said, without looking up from the paper. "I'm staying."

"I'll go then." Peri's mom hesitated, hand on the door to the garage. She shifted awkwardly from foot to foot. "Vicki's mom called last night."

Al and Peri both looked up.

"She said the police had called her about Vicki's case. She said the people that took Peri were the same people who took Vicki? Something about a brand being the same. I'm not sure I want to know what that means. But anyway, the police think it was the same people."

Al looked at Peri, who nodded. "Yeah," said Al, "they were."

"Well, um, she wanted to say thank you, so I gave her your address."

"What?" Al looked pissed.

"Not your actual address. I didn't think you'd like that. I gave her your P.O. Box. She said she wanted to write a letter."

Al looked at Peri, at a loss for words.

"That's a good idea. Thanks, Mom," whispered Peri.

"OK, good. I'll go then." Her mom took one last look at the two of them and then finally left.

Peri ate her sludge of a cereal, which was about the only thing that felt OK on her throat besides popsicles. The TV was playing another loop of the same news story. Peri watched as her tear-streaked face flashed across the screen for the umpteenth time, Emma and the other girls crowding around, flanked by cops as they were escorted away from the U-Haul lot. Then Al's hand pushed the camera away. The news shows hadn't figured out how to cut away before then. Maybe they liked Al's aggressively protective maneuver. Maybe they thought it made them look tough. Either way, the clip ended, and the news anchor came back on to reiterate that no names of the victims would be released because they were all underage. So far, no one had mentioned the involvement of any gangsters or local bowling alley employees. The newscasters were hailing Al as a hero. His military photo flashed on the screen. He looked so clean-cut and so young.

Al angrily changed the channel to a game show and went back to reading the paper.

Peri continued to eat as Al snuck a look at her over the top of the paper.

He cleared his throat. "You know you can't see him again, right?"

Peri stared at him.

"You were on the front page of the paper, and you've been all over the news for three days. You're too recognizable."

"Too recognizable for who?" she asked, pushing back.

"For his friends in the city. You know, the ones he specifically didn't call to come get you. The ones he doesn't want to know about you."

Peri looked down at her cereal. She had been hoping he wouldn't say it. "Yeah, I know."

"It's for the best," he said, sounding desperate. "You don't need somebody like that. You need a nice boy who will treat you good. That Trey kid was nice."

Peri stared at Al and tried to think through the mush and come up with words that would make Al understand.

"Trey is nice and I love him. But I don't need nice. I need someone who can keep up."

Al looked distressed. "You're going to go to college. You can stop all of this. You need to stop before you get hurt. I'm not fucking losing anyone else."

"Relax, Al," she said, standing up and taking her bowl to the sink. "You said it yourself. I'm burned. I'm too recognizable to do anyone any good. The magic wand has been waved. You get your wish. Poof, I'm retired."

Shark: The Beginning

Ryan was waiting for Shark in a hipster café on the West Side. The entire place was covered in green shamrocks. A chalkboard sign proclaimed all Irish specials. St. Patrick's Day was hitting the neighborhood with both barrels.

"I figured you might like this place better than IHOP," Ryan said as Shark sat down.

He looked around at the Edison lightbulbs and the bearded bartender who was fixing a just-so Bloody Mary while wearing a vest. The vest didn't even look like part of the uniform—unless it came standard issue with the beard. "Because twenty-dollar artisan burgers sound like my thing?"

"Were you born an asshole or do you practice every morning?"

"Both," said Shark, grinning.

"You shouldn't be smiling. The bureau is pissed as hell about the mess you made up at Harry Johnson's."

"That was out of my control. I called it in."

"A little too late," said Ryan.

"You know why," said Shark.

"Yeah, I do. You didn't want Vivian getting wind of it. Meanwhile, your private investigator friend is making you, and more importantly, the Bureau, look good on the U-Haul lot thing. Way to keep the scales balanced."

"He is not my friend," said Shark. "In fact, he pretty much hates me."

"Doesn't matter," said Ryan. "Only makes it better, really. Now, if you can just bring us Geier's head on a platter, you'll be in business."

"What about Vivian?" asked Shark. "When are you getting rid of her?"

"Ah," said Ryan. "Slight problem with that."

"What problem? You've got Peccary and Javelina. You've got their books. You've got everything. What else do you need?"

"Yeah, we've got all that, and we're making arrests all over the city. But Vivian isn't one of them."

"She's dirty! How are you not arresting her?"

"You misunderstand. She's dirty as fucking hell. Once we started digging, we just started tripping over shit. But it's a lot of little dirt—nothing big. And what we don't have is any connection between her and Preston Peccary. We don't want to arrest her yet because we don't know who she's working for. That's what we need you to find out."

Shark stared at Ryan in disbelief. "I'm so fucked."

"Yeah, kind of," said Ryan. "You want that burger now?"

SHARK'S FIN

When Shark Santoyo made a deal with the FBI to gather evidence against Geier, the boss of his old gang, he thought he'd be done in a few weeks. But six months later Shark is faced with an FBI handler who is working against him, an increasingly suspicious and erratic Geier and the fact that someone wants him dead. Shark is determined to be done with Geier and the FBI. Shark has only one goal in mind, and that's make it out of this mess alive, and make it back to the only girl who has ever held his trust and his heart—Peregrine Hays. But threats from within the gang and without have the net drawing ever tighter. This may be one trap he won't be able to swim away from.

Shark's Fin Sneak Peek...

Three Weeks Ago

Peregrine: College

Eighteen-year-old high school senior Peregrine Hays was fully retired. She was certain of it because no one had tried to kill her lately. The same could not be said of the lanky college student across the parking lot.

As she watched, a heavily muscled 'roid user stabbed at the pale kid stepping out of a Lexus. On instinct the boy, his arms full of books, turned toward his attacker and the knife lodged into a text book.

"I can't believe that you're not going to school with Trey in California," said Sarah, then followed the direction of Peri's gaze. "What the hell? Hey!"

The boy was now half-kneeling between two cars and the bigger man was standing over him. The man, put his foot on the book and pushed away, extracting a knife from where it had been impaled through the pages. The boy scrambled to his feet, and started to run. The bigger man gave chase.

"I mean you and Trey have been together forever," said Sarah, beckoning to the boy.

Peri waited for the right moment and considered the problem of her boyfriend. Treyvonne Smith was adorable, pre-med, and currently located in California because she had arranged for his drug-dealing uncle to be killed in a drive-by shooting.

"Run!" The boy yelled at them, taking his own advice. Neither Peri or Sarah moved.

"What did Trey say when you told him?" asked Sarah. The boy had almost reached them.

Peri and Sarah had worked together on the handful of occasions when Peri's work took her to Sacred Heart Catholic Girls School where Sarah Pearson and her younger sister had been students. The Pearson's biological father was their mother's one regret in life, a decent street magician, and three-card monte operator. As a result of weekends with her father, Sarah was handy in the pick-pocket department and shared Peri's rather flexible outlook on legality and morality. Peri and Sarah weren't particularly close, but Peri felt that their working relationship deserved a level of honesty that she might not have given others.

"I actually haven't told Trey yet," said Peri, hefting her bag. She saw Sarah's face. "I'm going to. I'm going out to see him in a few weeks. I just figure it's more of an in person conversation."

"Run! Run!" The boy yelled as he sprinted past. Peri stepped out and swung her backpack into his pursuer's face. The boy skidded to a halt and looked around at the sound of impact. His attacker tried to scramble off the ground, preparing to charge. But Peri kicked out into his groin, forcing him back down. Then she stomped on his knee. He bellowed in pain.

"Beat it, asshole" said Sarah, "The cops are on their way." She waved her phone, but hadn't actually dialed. She knew Peri's dislike for involving law enforcement. Clutching his groin, the man tried to crab walk backwards, then climbed to his feet and limped away.

"It's cool," said Sarah. "I'm just surprised. I think everyone figured you'd go out there to be with him."

"Well, I thought about it," said Peri. "But Stanford is Trey's dream, not mine. And my family is here. Not to mention out-of-state tuition is a bit of a killer."

"Sure," said Sarah, nodding. "And your work. It would probably be difficult to start up in a new state." Sarah turned to the boy before Peri could correct her. Not that she would have known what to say.

The truth was that she loved Trey, but she had stopped being *in love* with him the moment Shark Santoyo had entered her life. And the second truth was that if she wasn't working, she was no longer of any use to Shark. Which made her forced retirement even more bitter and her decision to attend the local university even more inexplicable. She couldn't explain that she had stayed for the very thin hope that she might see Shark. She couldn't explain that to anyone, because after all, she had her pride. But her pride did not stop her from wanting Shark any more than it could stop her from checking every phone call and text with a spike of hope that was immediately flattened.

"What the hell was that, Kyle?" demanded Sarah.

Kyle looked to be in his early twenties, gangly, with a shock of brown hair and a gamer's pale complexion.

"I don't know!" he gasped, still breathing heavily. "He just came out of nowhere and tried to stab me."

"You really ought to pay your gambling debts," said Peri, who recognized a leg-breaker when she saw one. "People get peevy when you don't."

"I don't have any," he panted.

"Are you sure?" asked Sarah skeptically.

"I can't make book in this town," said Kyle, shaking his head. "My uncle won't let me."

Peri frowned. There was always a bookie somewhere who would take a bet. Kyle must not have tried very hard.

"Well, in that case," said Sarah, looking back at Peri, "I guess that concludes the most exciting college orientation tour ever. I'm not sure why you would want to attend with Kyle here as a recommendation, but welcome to university life."

"I swear it's not usually like this!" exclaimed Kyle.

"It's fine," said Peri with a shrug.

"No, it's not! I can't believe you guys aren't freaking out. That guy was major scary!"

"Peri has a high tolerance for other people's fear," said Sarah.

"And Sarah's just badass," said Peri.

"I guess so," said Kyle, shaking his head. "Thanks a bunch for helping out." He looked around, clearly at a loss for what to do next. "I was supposed to hit the library for some studying, but that is so not happening. Can I buy you guys a beer or something? I'm Kyle, by the way."

"Kyle Geier," said Sarah, "meet Peregrine Hays. She helps people solve problems."

"Not anymore," said Peri. "I'm retired."

Find out what happens next in...

SHARK'S FIN

Dear Reader,

Word-of-mouth is crucial for any author to succeed. If you enjoyed the book, please leave a review on Amazon. Even if it's just a sentence or two. It would make all the difference and would be very much appreciated:

www.amazon.com, search for: *Bethany Maines*

Thank you!

ABOUT THE AUTHOR

Bethany Maines is the award-winning author of action adventure and fantasy tales that focus on women who know when to apply lipstick and when to apply a foot to someone's hind end. When she's not traveling to exotic lands, or kicking some serious butt with her black belt in karate, she can be found chasing after her daughter, or glued to the computer working on her next novel.

ALSO BY BETHANY MAINES

CARRIE MAE MYSTERIES
Bulletproof Mascara
Compact With The Devil
High-Caliber Concealer
Glossed Cause

SAN JUAN ISLANDS MYSTERIES
An Unseen Current
Against the Undertow
An Unfamiliar Sea
An Unfinished Storm

SHARK SANTOYO CRIME SERIES
Shark's Instinct
Shark's Bite
Shark's Hunt
Shark's Fin
Peregrine's Flight
Shark's Blood

THE DEVERAUX LEGACY
The Second Shot
A PNWA Literary ContesttAward Winner
The Cinderella Secret
The Hardest Hit
The Fallen Man

THE SUPERNATURALS
Wild Waters
A Little Red (3 Colors #1)
A Deeper Blue (3 Colors #2)
A Brighter Yellow (3 Colors #3)
Maverick
Hudson (Rejects #1)
Killian (Rejects #2)
Alekos (Rejects #3)

GALACTIC DREAMS
When Stars Take Flight Vol. 1
The Seventh Swan Vol. 2
A Book Excellence Award Winner
The Beast of Arsu Vol. 3

Find out more at:
BethanyMaines.com